EXILE

KEITH MURPHY URBAN FANTASY THRILLERS

Gold Coast Ragnarök Trilogy

EXILE

Keith Murphy flees a hit gone wrong, smuggling out a ghost trapped in a bullet with the potential to end the world. Staying safe means doing a deal with a devil holding on to an old grudge.

FROST

Keith's caught up in a gang war between the local bikers and his demonic ex-boss, but there's something far more dangerous lurking out in the cold.

CRUSADE

Ragnarök comes to the Gold Coast and Keith Murphy's the only man who can stop it. All he's got to do is trust a seer who seems anything but trustworthy.

Keith Murphy Singles

LOCAL HEROES

A demon using the wrestling ring to steal power from mortal fans. Keith Murphy takes him on to pay off a major debt, and learns there's more to this demon than meets the eye.

EXILE

A KEITH MURPHY URBAN FANTASY THRILLER

PETER M. BALL

Brain Jar Press
PO Box 6687
Upper Mt Gravatt, QLD, 4122
Australia
www.BrainJarPress.com

Cover design by Brain Jar Press
Cover Image: Contract Killer, lassedesignen; ancient runic magic symbol,
longquatro; viking rune symbol, longquatro/Shutterstock

ISBN: 978-0-6481761-6-9

CONTENTS

PARADISE CITY

They found me in the Hard Rock. Thursday night, a little after ten. The bar drew a good crowd for a Thursday, all things considered. Lots of girls with inscrutable, backpacker accents clustered around the counter. Plenty more heading for the Beer Garden upstairs, attracted by the cover band's caterwaul. Blondes, legitimate and peroxide — a Gold Coast epidemic. Swathes of exposed skin, despite the cool nip in the air. Twenty-dollar cocktails named after natural disasters: Typhoons; Tsunamis; rum-soaked Hurricanes.

I'd racked up three straight hours sitting in the downstairs bar, drinking short blacks and reading my book. A guy flying solo at at a cozy table for four, ignoring the crush of the late-night crowd, the heady mingling of sweat and perfume and the salt-water from the nearby beach. I blew off the irritated, dark-eyed waitress who kept offering to take my coffee cup in the hopes I'd fuck off and free up the four top. I wasn't waiting for anyone else. Just me and my beat-up copy of *Persuasion* on yet another stake-out, killing time until the local talent picked up on my presence.

I'd selected a table up the back, wedged between one of Keith Moon's polyester shirts and Mark Occhilupo's surfboards. Earlier, when I'd been eating dinner, tourists stopped by to read the brass plaques and sniff at my empty seats. Personally, I didn't give a shit about the memorabilia. My position delivered clear sight-lines on the bar, the gift shop, and both sets of sliding doors.

The band working upstairs distracted me with their off-key singing and affection for the Gunners. Every time they launched into another cover, I'd lose my place and have to re-read the same page of *Persuasion* again. I'd stumbled over the same line about fine ladies and calm waters ever since their version of 'Knocking on Heaven's Door.' They were leading the bellicose crowd through the chorus of 'Paradise City' right as the demon walked in.

His arrival marked the end of my reading. I downed the dregs of my coffee and watched the big feller work. The purposeful stroll through the gift shop, all swagger and white teeth. The momentary pause as he scanned the room with a jungle cat's poise, making a note of every warm body crammed in among the memorabilia. I figured him for six-nine, give or take an inch. Athletic and well-built, dressed to fit in with the local crowd. Tight black jeans and bright red high-top sneakers, a walnut tan just brown enough to be real instead of spray-on.

The kind of guy I'd remember, even after sixteen years, and I couldn't recall anyone with his height and frame among Sabbath's mooks. New blood, then. Definitely a demon. I didn't need to pierce the veil to confirm it — he carried himself in that languid, unsettling way most creatures of the Gloom deploy when they forget to play human.

The short, dark-eyed waitress stopped by my table and removed the empty coffee cup. Asked me if I'd like another, and broke into a grin when I told her I'd finish up soon. I pulled a twenty out of my wallet, folded it, and slid it beneath the salt and pepper shakers. Dog-eared my current page and stuffed *Persuasion* into a jacket pocket so I wouldn't leave it behind. Things would start moving fast now a demon was on the prowl.

He crossed the bar at a leisurely pace, stopped to chat up women and deploy a toothy smile. The first three shot him down, which took effort on his part. Demons flirt easier than most people breathe, and this guy's jaw and build were easy on the eyes. In the fourth he found a receptive partner, the kind of chick young men dream of meeting at a joint like the Hard Rock: bleached-blond; white t-shirt; tanned and smooth and friendly, her cut-off jeans showing off the pink hibiscus tattooed on her right thigh. Her intentions were obvious in the raucous laugh she deployed, and her drunken lurch into the demon's side.

Then the Big Guy glanced my way, a surreptitious glance to confirm I'd clocked his presence. Could be a subtle warning to back off and let him feed in peace, or a predator recognizing a potential threat and disregarding it before hunting. And so we kicked off a round of my least-favorite game, trying to figure who was playing who.

The blonde made it easy for the Big Guy. Pressed against him, whispered into his ear. Midriff top giving him access to bare skin as he pulled her close. The veins closest to his fingertips turned dark as he siphoned a fragment of her life-force. He did it light and subtle, like a pickpocket filching your wallet. The drain left the girl woozy, bought the demon a chance to prop her against the bar and scan the crowd for another victim.

Slick work, and feeding in public is brazen for any demon. This guy played it cool, focused on the prey. My presence forgotten or disregarded, confident I wouldn't risk a move on Sabbath's turf and put a target on my back. Given the way possession enhanced human senses, he already knew I wasn't local. My scent was fresh off the Greyhound, a sour-and-rumpled traveler who'd gone too long without sleep. My flannel shirt too warm for the Gold Coast summer, but ideal for covering the the tethers inked along my arm and the SIG tucked into my belt.

I tracked his movements, trying to figure out if he was overconfident, dumb, or extremely good. Realized too late he was the fourth option: a big, distracting billboard deployed to capture my attention. When the .38 kissed the hollow of my back, just below the ribs, a part of me was flattered I'd warranted that kind of caution from two alpha predators.

Of course, that part of me was dumb as rocks, but I guess nobody's perfect.

Wesna Holjack leaned over my right shoulder, her voice tickling my ear. "Well, shit, Keith Murphy. How the fuck are you?"

"Hey Wes," I said. "Been a while, yeah?"

"You think?" She slid into the empty seat beside me, draped her arm around my neck. The other hand jammed the pistol into my gut, made it clear trying to squirm or run would trigger a messy response.

"You should have left it longer," Wesna said. "Now I'm kinda pissed I have to kill you."

I knew I'd fucked up, the moment I heard Wesna's voice. Desperation will do that to you.

Sixteen years back, Wesna Holjack was a friend. A tall girl, tough as boiled leather. Determined to carve out a reputation as one of the guys at our high school, less concerned with surfer kids than the motley crew of freaks who accepted her penchant for violence. She boxed and fought Muay Thai for a stretch, kicked more ass than any kid in our class.

The Wesna Holjack beside me, sixteen years later, matched the girl in my memory exactly. Same black hair hanging over her face. Same long, bulldog jaw designed to take a punch and let her keep on ticking. Same irritation in her eyes, the look that said she'd caught me fucking up yet again and resigned herself to covering my ass. Problem was, the Wesna Holjack digging her .38 into my ribs still looked about twenty-three.

The possessed don't age like ordinary people. It's one perk demons used to con you into offering your body as a timeshare. Plenty of folks accept the deal, realize too late their humanity gets strip-mined away and the demon gets to walk around in their place. Wesna might not be that far gone, but any memories of our friendship were suspect. I played it safe, spread my hands on the table. Kept them clear of anything that might constitute a potential weapon.

Wesna leaned over to nuzzle against my neck, feigning affection we'd never shared. She cracked her gum in my ear and exhaled, drawing goosebumps on my traitorous arms as my body responded to her proximity. "Here's the deal," Wesna said, the barrel of the .38 steady as a rock against my ribs. "You play along, and I don't shoot you here. We have ourselves a conversation, all nice and private-like, and you keep breathing until we're done."

Wesna threatened with confidence, utterly capable of following through. I buttoned my lip, both hands palm-down on the table. Experience taught me the value of gathering intel, and right now I needed to gauge Wesna's self-control.

Her reaction to my silence was a long way from her boiling point. Wesna ground the gun barrel into my flank. "Tell me you understand, Murphy, or I ventilate your ass."

"I know the routine, Wes. Jesus."

Her dark eyes flicked over my face, eerily calm and unimpressed with my response. "If that were true, you wouldn't blaspheme."

"Good advice. I'll keep that in mind."

Wesna glanced at the Big Guy, over by the bar, and the second demon acknowledged her with a nod. He ordered a beer and slouched against the counter, eyes fixed on me and nauseatingly smug. "Your partners smarter than he looks," I said.

"Randall has that going for him."

I twitched my hands, drawing Wesna's attention to me. "I'm armed. SIG in my waistband, around the back."

Wesna's hand slid down, slow and professional. She found the gun, pulled it free. Consigned it to the small handbag slung over her shoulder. "Anything else?"

I took a long, silent breath and shook my head. Confirmed my vulnerability, although she doubted the truth of it. Wesna checked out the other patrons, searching for weapons or gathered power. "Can't see a second out there. That ain't like you."

"I'm flying solo here," I said. "Not on the job. Not looking for a fight."

I counted off the seconds as Wesna chewed that over. Watched her do the math, puzzle out the implications of trying to prove me wrong. Hauling me out by here would get very public, and demons aren't fond of scrutiny at the best of times. Accepting my word meant risking the possibility I was lying and my own ambush lay in the wings.

She looked at me. I looked at her. Wesna idled her way to a plan of action. "I'm putting the gun away," she said. "A favor for an old friend, yeah? I'd rather not drag you out of here at gunpoint, so if you're willing to behave…"

There was a long pause as she studied my face, and I did my best to appear contrite and harmless. The .38 ceased pressing against my spleen, disappeared into the depths of Wesna's jacket. My spleen shivered with relief and the rest of me followed suite. Wesna shifted to the far side of the table, poised like a serpent waiting for a cornered mouse to break and flee.

I let my vision shift past the real world, piercing the veil to glimpse Wesna's face in the shadows of the Gloom. Not my favorite activity—I'd spent years suppressing a natural talent for breaching the facade we call reality—and the split focus took its toll. But when I concentrated on Wesna Holjack, familiar features gave way to a husk ravaged by prolonged possession. Mortal eyes decayed to hollow sockets with a crimson fire in their depths. Her skin burned dark and ashen, the scraps of her human spirit little more than bright pocks of sulfurous light waging a futile war against the darker presence in charge of the body.

The headache thundered in, right on schedule. The effort of piercing the veil of the Gloom extracting its price. Wesna recognized the signs from our teenage years. "That was incredibly stupid," she said.

"Yeah. I'm aware," I said.

"I should be calling Sabbath. He'll be overjoyed your bitch-ass was dumb enough to come home."

"You think?"

"Definitely."

"Best you get on with that, then."

My agreement caught Wesna off guard, fired up her suspicion I might be playing some longer game. She flicked a glance at the doors and her big, good-looking back-up.

She eased forward and dropped her voice. "Stop trying to be a hard-ass, Murphy. Give me a reason to let you walk, here," she said. For a moment I glimpsed the woman she'd been, struggling her way to the surface.

A smile bloomed across my lips, ready to welcome her. Not a bright idea if I wanted to keep on living. I forced the nostalgia down with a vengeance. "Sorry, Wes. I got nothing."

"Murphy, come on. Work with me."

I folded my arms and looked to the Big Guy. He'd reared up, intrigued by our conversation and its departure from the expected. Ready to come in if I started trouble. I shook my head, turned back to Wesna. "Guess you'd better call, eh? Be a good little soldier?"

"Fuck you," she said, and the phone was in her hand.

Wesna searched my face for tells, waiting for me to give her something. We both remembered the threats Sabbath made when I left, and the price of coming home. Wesna ground her teeth and flared her nostrils, hissing like a kettle.

I kept both hands flat and waited. The band in the upstairs bar continued their tour through the best of Guns and Roses, segueing from "Sweet Child of Mine" into "November Rain". Their guitarist could play, but the singer just liked to wail. Good enough for a Thursday night, though. All the crowd demanded was volume and the chance to sing along.

I jerked my chin at the stairwell, risked invoking a little history. "You remember when Nora drove us all to Byron and *Use Your Illusion* was the only tape in the car?"

Wesna snorted her disdain, but it seemed to push her towards a decision. "Lot of noise in this bar," she said. "Hard to hear, you know what I'm saying? Think I'll step outside to make this call. Should be, what, five minutes? Ten? Boss can slow to answer his phone, this time of night."

The demon clawed and yowled behind her dark, terrible stare. A part of Wesna's humanity just marshaled its resources to fight on my behalf, deploying a few scraps of mercy against the demon's better judgment. She'd offered me a chance to avoid the torrents of shit coming my way.

It broke my heart that I needed to throw it all back in her face. "I appreciate the offer, but call Sabbath from here. I'm not running, Wes. The boss and I need to converse about things."

Wesna swore, her jaw pulling tight. "He ain't eager to talk, Murphy. And he ain't your boss."

"Then you may as well pull the trigger."

She blew a long, frustrated breath. Dialed a number from memory and waited for someone to answer.

"Yeah," she said. "It's me."

Her eyes stayed on me, hoping like hell I'd change my mind and bolt.

"It's definitely him," she said. Then: "Yeah, I can do that."

She killed the call with her thumb, returned the phone to her jacket. Turned and signaled the Big Guy, waving him over to our table. He broke off from the backpacker he'd been chatting up, became a tall, good-looking shark cutting through the press of bodies. Up close, I could make out biceps and pecs testing the physical limits of shirt. Impressive to look at, but the big man's grace was the real threat. "This is Randall," Wesna said. "He'll be escorting you."

Randall exposed his teeth. A feral, eager smile.

"Randall, Keith Murphy. Don't let the odor fool you."

Randall's eyebrows shot up at my name. "Well, shit. I've heard of you, man."

I swung free of the table and stared up at him. "Good things, I hope?"

"Outstanding things." The big demon cracked his knuckles. "It's been ages since I tortured somebody."

DOUBLE-TAP

They walked me towards the door as a unit: Randall took point, sticking close enough to block my retreat, making sure none of the Hard Rock bouncers tried to get to help. Wesna right beside me, feigning inebriation, one arm slung across my shoulder and her voice slurring in my ear. At the exit, Randall went out first, waited for Wesna to push me through. Careful, efficient moves to keep me locked down.

Outside, on the crowded street, the humidity pressed down on us like a sweat-soaked rag over your mouth. The kind of vile and muggy heat that made the short list of reasons why I'd been overjoyed to leave the Coast and never come back. Emerging into it, after the air conditioning, took my breath away. Even Wesna straightened, unwilling to make anymore contact than was necessary given the way I perspired. That was a good sign. It meant she trusted the signs I wasn't going to run.

The neon guitar over the Hard Rock entrance soaked the street in whisky-colored light. We were on the corner of Orchid and Cavill Ave, a perpetually crowded intersection where cars and pedestrians swore at one another and fought for right of way. The press of bodies made running impossible, and I figured the demons could track me even if I'd been inclined to try. Wesna frowned and considered the flow of drunks, the oppressive heat, and my compliance. She pointed at the wall. "You wait."

I took a spot with my back to beige concrete, and Randall stepped over to pen me in. A slick, natural move like we were trying to talk over the crowd noise, decide which club to hit next. It put him between me and any real avenue of escape, and that wasn't coincidental.

"Watch him," Wesna said. "I'll call us a ride, yeah?"

Things I understood, coming back to the Gold Coast, that I hadn't known before I left: There are fourteen reliable methods of killing a body possessed by a demon, but that number drops the longer the demon's been in residence. There are six effective techniques for eliminating the fey once they leave the Gloom and dwell in our reality. Eight ways of taking out a lycanthrope, if you're not picky about saving the human half, and myriad approaches to disposing of sorcerers and witches after you've bypassed the protective magic they've used to keep themselves alive.

None of those things are easy, and they all get a hell of a lot harder for mortals without Gloom-touched powers of their own. Botch an attempt, and shit goes hideously wrong. The kind of wrong that gets folks killed. The kind of wrong that means you're working without back-up, and the nightmares of your childhood are free to haunt you again.

The whisky-colored light of the Hard Rock's neon guitar lent Randall's tan an unhealthy, sallow cast. I doubt it did me any favors either, the way I sweated now we were out.

"As I understand it," Randall said, "you're not one of Sabbath's favorite people."

I made a non-committal noise, gave nothing away. Wesna pushed through the crowd and took a position by the curb, her phone pressed against her left ear. Standard operating procedure for Sabbath's crew, dealing with an incursion. Shuffle the newcomer off the street and hide him from prying mortals. Once upon a time, I'd been the guy making the call and fretting, keeping one eye on the subject in case they bolted for freedom.

"Never met someone the boss outright hates." Randall pitched his voice just below the hubbub of the crowd, pressed his weight forward to lock me down and make sure I caught every word. "Ordinarily, he's all, you know, all business. No time for grudges or nothing." He puffed out his cheeks, exhaled slowly. "Way he acted when your name came up, when we heard you were here, just eating a burger…"

Randall waited for a reaction, but I didn't rise to the bait. Not worth it. I studied the road instead. Randall shook his head, fighting back a smile. "Boss ain't never talked like that," he said. "Man has a grudge against you, Murphy."

The lights at the intersection turned green and the crowd surged across the street. A flow of revelers from either side, a late night tide of clubbers and drunks and tourists searching for the next party. The constant din of bodies and chatter, shouted conversations and music bleeding out of passing cars and nearby clubs. A knot of chaos and transience, every part thrumming with energy. Even without the press of the Gloom, it would have given me a headache.

I gazed into the chaotic mass, trying to make sense of it. My conscious brain was busy negotiating the problems of being back home again, but my subconscious still tracked the world around me and it recognized a greater hazard in my vicinity than an irritated demon and his vindictive boss.

Randall blathered on regardless. "You know how long it's been since Sabbath gave me the all-clear to really *hurt* a man?"

There was nothing pleasant behind Randall's pristine smile, just the implied threat of how bad things would get if I kept on trying to blank him. At my best, I might have put on a show for him, played for time and information. Instead, I gave him a half-hearted response. "A while, I'm guessing?"

"A good, long while." He eased forward, planted his palm beside my head. "Shit, man, this is like goddamn Christmas for us, you know?"

I switched back to the street and the crowd, Wesna still talking on her phone. "Yeah, I remember the drill."

Randall grinned and inched closer, crowding me up against the wall. "Tonight's shaping up to be a good night, mate. A real good night, indeed."

I said nothing in reply.

"Unless the boss wants to get his hands dirty." Randall squinted, considering the implications. He wanted the change of tack to disorient me, start me thinking about greater threats. I'd worked that schtick myself in the past. It's one of Sabbath's favorites. Randall handled it well enough, dropped his voice to a breathy, eager whisper. "Even then, I'm guessing I make do with observing. Almost as good, watching, you know?"

I tuned the demon out and scanned the crowd, no longer concerned with being subtle. Randall failed to notice. "You smell like ass," he said. "Hope the boss hoses you down 'fore we go to work on you and all."

"Shut-up," I said. "Your four o'clock."

Randall squinted, confused. Turned around a fraction slower than he would have, if he paid attention.

Which meant he didn't see the sorcerer until it was too damn late.

He loitered in the crowd, blending in with the tourists and late night drinkers heading for the next stop on a binge. Mid-thirties, maybe—the beard made his age hard to peg down. Tight black t-shirt over a broad, surfer's chest. Every inch a local old-boy, still cruising the clubs and hitting on younger chicks, one of the endless tide of low-key assholes who infested the Cavill Ave nightlife. He put effort into the image, but the tattoos gave him away. They ran down the soft parts of his inner forearm, the runes partially disguised by the Chinese dragon that wound between them.

They were tether marks, allowing him to touch into the Gloom, use it for things ordinary people would end up calling magic. I figured he'd been there a few hours, long enough to tap the shadows and drawing out what he needed to do some damage. He must've bloodied his hand at the start of that, left it dripping slow and steady as he drew in power. When he saw Randall jerk around, he guessed his cover was a blown. Which meant it was time to make a move and deploy all that energy siphoned from the Gloom while he stood there being a creepy fucker.

Shadows swam over him as he pulled the Gloom into our world, tenebrous strands of darkness reaching from beneath parked cars and the weird angles cast by the neon. On a street full of people coming and going, he focused on staying still, drawing the umbral energies together until time seemed too slow.

He stood on the corner, shoulder pressed against the building. Held a smoke with his left hand, never pulling it far from his face. His right arm dangled at his side, clenched tight, blood dripping through his fingers.

It took effort, dragging that much of the Gloom into our world, binding it into something you could use as a weapon. The air hummed with the potential of it, blended with the rhythms of the ocean just two blocks away.

The sorcerer on the corner flicked his cigarette into the gutter, raised the bloodied fist.

I grabbed Wesna by the arm, hauled her to the ground.

Her phone shattered against concrete and Randall lunged for me, still unsure about my motives. Realized his mistake as a black inferno speared through the crowd. The attack caught Randall in the chest, knocked him onto his ass. The dark mockery of fire clung to him, burning through his shirt.

Randall writhed, desperately beating at the unnatural flames. The pedestrians parted like the red sea, bodies surging backwards to escape the immolation. I reached for my SIG on instinct, realized the pistol now occupied Wesna's bag. She kicked away from me and rose with her snub-nosed .32 in hand. Her steady grip tracked the weapon towards the sorcerer, picked the right moment to unleash lead. Wesna's finger tightened against the trigger, two shots in quick succession. Shot one ricocheted. The second caught the target in the right arm, digging deep into the muscle.

More blood on the concrete. More screams from the crowd.

The sorcerer just laughed.

The first order of business: escape and evade. Long experience taught me sorcerers are a bitch to kill with hand weapons, especially when you don't have your own sorcerer to counter them, and they're a considerably worse proposition if you wound them without finishing the job. Wesna emptied her weapon, pumping another seven rounds into our attacker. Not trying to slay him, just slow him down. Force him to use magic to heal the injuries instead of blasting us with fire.

"Up." Wesna knelt beside me, sliding a new clip home. The sorcerer sagged against the wall, blood staining his shirt. Randall's wet breathing cut through the air. I rolled over, got my feet under me.

There were cops coming down the street, from the patrol that worked the nearby mall. The shouted orders, telling everyone to get down. Randall crawled to his knees, chest still burning. Wesna grabbed him, hauled the bigger demon over one shoulder. She glanced my way, eyes hard as stone.

"I think we should run," she said.

No argument from me. I lurched into motion, barging through the crowd. Wesna lugged Randal after me, barking orders and trusting good sense to keep me obeying. Unarmed and without back-up, there weren't many other choices open to me.

She led us south, away from the club distract and the crowds giving the sorcerer cover. Away from the barked orders as cops arrived and the sirens right behind them, back-up responding to the fire and reports of shot fired.

Behind us the sorcerer stepped into the Gloom and disappeared, no more eager to deal with authorities than Wesna, Randal, or I.

BREATHER

We took refuge in a dinky little Thai place three blocks down from the Hard Rock. One of those hole in the wall joints, perpetually empty and around forever. Every city has 'em. Part of you wonders how they stay in business, when you deign to give 'em a moment's thought. Most days, they float beneath your radar. Either way, you don't go in. That's cool. The things that run those restaurants prefer to have vacant tables.

Wesna positioned us by the front window, a four-seater with a good view of the sirens rolling past. The red and blue lights cut through the Gloom-tinged streets, cops swarming in to expand the perimeter as they sought the folks involved in the shooting. Wesna scanned the traffic and sidewalk, looking for signs of a tail. I waited, content to let her run the play, no point in drawing more attention than we'd already received.

It was coming up on eleven PM, right on closing time. The restaurant empty of everyone but the three of us, and the gray-haired bloke in a natty suit who worked the front of house. He'd taken one look at Randall and flipped the sign to closed, a quick conversation with Wesna confirming we'd be okay to lie low for a stretch.

The owner disappeared into the kitchen and returned with some half-eaten plates of food, laying them out like we'd been demolishing a feast for the better part of an hour. Job done, he'd turned to Wesna and asked a question in his native Thai. Wesna responded in kind, kept her answers short. The old bloke glanced at me, glanced at Randall; shook his head as he retreated to the back of house, bellowing at his employees. Wesna perched on the edge of her seat, peering through the glass window. Randall slumped in the chair beside her, drawing wheezy breathes as he prodded the blistered skin on his chest. "Fucking hell, that hurt," he repeated.

Wesna told him to shut up, but Randall merely dropped his complaints to a whisper. Demons heal fast, encouraging human biology to work at a speed it couldn't do on its own, drawing on the Gloom to catalyse the added pace. They also like to bitch while it happens. My own ribs ached from the quick sprint. I steadied my breathing, trying to slow it down.

"He doesn't sound happy," I said, nodding at the kitchen doors.

"Ben's an old friend," she said. "But he dislikes disruption. Too much attention."

"I know your old friends, Wes'. I used to be one of them."

Wesna's head jerked towards me, her finger raised in anger. She held it there, about to tee off, but the tirade didn't come. She glanced at Randall, then back at the kitchen. Clenched her fingers and lowered her hand to the tabletop.

A few blocks up the cops were cleaning up outside the Hard Rock, trying to figure out exactly what occurred. The stories from the crowd wouldn't be much help. They'd be hazy about what started the fire, reports about Molotov's conflicting with those who figured Randall spontaneously combusted. Everybody would mention a chick with a gun, but the details would never matched up. Humanity's ability to rationalize the impossible is imperfect, but reliable.

Wesna wasn't working with the same handicap as the

cops. Eventually she'd figure out I was the target. I didn't want that. Negotiating with people who wish you dead is harder when they think you've brought trouble onto their patch.

Offense beat defense. "You guys been having problems with locals again?"

That earned me an angry look. "How 'bout you shut up, Murphy."

"All I'm saying is, he looked like a local," I said. "Nothing wavered when you plugged him, so it probably wasn't glamor."

"And you're running," she said. "Fuck knows what from, but it's the only reason you'd come home."

"Not so."

"Last I heard, you were in Adelaide. You and your fucking partner."

"You ever seen the beaches in Adelaide, Wes? Only thing between you and the Antarctic ice is the occasional humpback whale. I got eager for a little break, and I knew the Coast would be warm,."

I dropped into silence, let her think. She brooded, hissing like a kettle as it comes off the boil. It wasn't long before her phone rang, drawing a scowl as she checked the number.

"Yeah?" She glared at me as her caller rattled off a query.

"Unavoidable," she said, and it sparked another period of waiting for a chance to speak. Her eyes stayed locked on me, cold and suspicious. "Yes, we picked him up."

Her face tightened at the response. Then: "No, I don't think that's the case."

I could see the fires burning in her pupils when she hung up. Not much of the woman I'd known remained once she got that pissed off. Demons rode negative emotions, used them to subvert the human soul. I grinned at Wesna, stoking the anger. The longer fury kept her distracted, the greater chance I could play things like the attack wasn't my fault.

"Sabbath still wants to see you," she said.

"You reckon he'll be understanding about the firefight that just went down?"

Wesna stood, hauling Randall to his feet with one hand. "No," she said, "he won't."

Wesna called a cab the moment the road started to clear. Randall glared at me as he healed, picking at the remnants of a chicken and cashew stir fry the old bloke delivered to us. I sat quietly and contemplated how much fucking trouble I was in.

The answer wasn't a happy one.

If you're wondering, this is how a guy like me ends up in situation this bad: it starts when he's young. You take an ordinary, middle-class kid from a nice, white middle-class family. You let him grow up in the suburbs of the Coast, send him to school with other nice, white kids, and pretend he's got a future. Then puberty hits at twelve, and brings with it more than a growth spurt, a breaking voice, and nocturnal emissions of the sexual kind. Puberty awakens his ability to peel back the veil, glimpse the world behind the world and the monsters that live among us.

Things fall apart.

People get antsy about the stories the kid tells. The kind of antsy that leads to psychologist appointments and the occasional antipsychotic. Eventually, the kind of antsy that leads to inefficient exorcisms and protective charms bought off the internet. None of it does shit to stop the kid seeing demons and monsters at every turn, but the kid's parents are so damned freaked out that bad things happen and nobody's coping.

So your kid runs away at fourteen. His parents don't go after him.

You trade the kid's nice, suburban life with a family of

misfit toys. Surround him with freaks and weirdoes, folks who brush against the monsters and lurk in the dark beside them. Eventually, the kid encounters a demon with ambitions. The demon recognizes the kid's got a natural talent, something to cultivate. They get him off the streets and back into school, grooming him for a bright future as muscle in their organization. He learns to shoot. He learns to mask his second-sight. He learns how to hurt people.

Your kid, he goes with it, because it's better than feeling crazy. Everybody wants to be part of something, and this seems like his best shot.

It starts easy, just identifying folks. This guy working the supermarket counter isn't human. This gal checking parking meters on the beach is Gloom-touched, and might be amenable to letting a demon inside her. Eventually, the jobs get harder. Your kid's a courier, transporting drugs and worse. He graduates to thug. Carries a big stick as well as a gun. The demons' organization grows. By seventeen, it's clear the kid's got a future. Not a bright future, but he's going somewhere. The demon owns the Gold Coast in every way that matters.

Then your kid meets a girl, and things fall apart all over again.

The girl ain't touched by the Gloom at all, and the kid doesn't want her to be part of that life. So now he's keeping secrets from the demon. He's lying to a woman he cares for. Swears he doesn't love her, because loving her would put her in all kinds of danger. Your kid tries to make up for all that with hard work. He's no longer the muscle, because the Demon needs a killer. The kid graduates to wet work, even though he doesn't love it.

All the lying takes its toll. Things fall apart, much worse than before.

The kid wonders if he could do in his life. Turns out, it's damned unlikely. He'll be this fucking asshole killer until he dies, or he agrees to let a demon cohabitate in his body. There's no future for him and the girl like that.

Then Danny Roark shows up. Offers to train the kid to save lives, even if he'll still be killing folks. A chance to become a hunter, instead of an assassin, and earn a little cash on the way.

It's a better choice than staying, so the kid goes with it. Walks away from his old boss, the demon. Walk away from the girl he might have loved. Danny Roark cuts a deal with the demon to ensure the kid doesn't spend his life looking over one shoulder.

The kid gives Roark sixteen years, specializing in killing entities from the realm sorcerers call the Gloom. Creatures who deserve a few bullets in the head, because their magic relies on death and corruption. The kid and Roark work out a system: Roark does the magic, the kid handles the guns.

Truth is, the split is rarely quite that clean, but the kid does what's necessary to make the partnership work. He's always done what's necessary. That's how he rolls.

And he's still killing folks, even if those folks aren't human. It's better, but it ain't ideal, and he's living life out of a suitcase. So he decides it's time to quit that life. Tells Roark, his partner, they're done.

Roark talks the kid into one last hit, picks this asshole down in Adelaide who *definitely* needs killing. The kid accepts the job, and it all goes down real smooth. They strip the target's defenses and put a bullet in him. Siphon off his soul and trap it, so the target can't disappear into the Gloom and resurrect himself.

The kid assumes it's finally done. Mission accomplished. Crusade over. Time to go live a real life.

Then he gets back to the safe house and Danny Roark is gone. The note on the coffee table says everything's gone to hell, and the kid knows what to do.

So he swallows a bullet with a soul stuffed inside and

hightails it out of Adelaide. Heads back to the one city where the Gloom's so thick and chaotic that tracking him with magic is damn near impossible.

Running doesn't bother him. Running's a survival trait.

What bothers him is running without having Roark for back-up. What bothers him is walking straight into a sorcerer's ambush, before he's clocked up his first twenty-four hours.

What bothers him is the nine millimeter bullet nestled in his intestines, the one with the soul of his last victim neatly trapped inside it. Walking into Sabbath's turf with nothing to bargain with, knowing he'll order the kid's death.

What bothers him is that it's never over, and he never gets to leave all this shit behind.

SABBATH

The cab deposited us at the front doors of Jupiter's Casino. Fifteen minute drive. Twenty-bucks on the meter. Wesna paid the cabbie, led me through the lobby. Randall stayed behind, his chest raw and blistered from the sorcerer's assault. Jupiter's is an open-minded place, the tuxedo crowd drinking alongside the country boys in flannel shirts and the hipsters from the local uni with their skinny jeans and lumberjack beards. Egalitarian by virtue of greed and the unity that comes from desperation and the white heat of waiting for the next spin. You could stretch the Gold Coast's permissive nature, but there were limits. The one rule nobody broke: no shirt, no shoes, no service. Even demons abided by it, went looking for another entrance.

The interior of the casino was blessedly cool, the open spaces dotted with palms and lounges and discretely placed security guards. They were big lads, suits and radio mics in place, predominantly human in heritage. The sole exception checked ID at the entrance to the Prince Albert pub, tucked in beside the elevators. He looked my way and flashed a sharp-toothed grin, eyes blazing with a crimson light.

Wesna snapped her glare towards him, and the security ghoul backed off a step. I fell in beside her. Casinos do their best to keep you from realizing the time, but my gut said Midnight was coming soon and there'd be a Gloom tide on its heels. The frenzied slurry of noise from the Prince Albert leaked into the lobby, indistinct and chaotic. The pub crowd skewed younger than the bars down by the gaming floor. More interested in drinking, less interested in blowing money on blackjack or power machines.

We settled in to wait for an elevator. Wesna leant against the wall, her eyes locked on me. It wasn't necessary—escape was impossible, once we stepped foot on casino grounds. Sabbath's name didn't appear on the deed, but he owned the place in every way that mattered. He'd bought in when they built, back in eighty-five. Clung on like a tick, feeding on the desperation that hung in the crisp, dry air they pumped through the complex, growing bloated and powerful.

The elevator came. We rode up in silence. The bell chimed, opened out onto a hallway extending in both directions. Twenty floors up. One below the penthouse suits. It's the way Sabbath played things, hovering below the level that drew notice. Display just enough importance to let you know he meant something, but avoid center stage.

Gold Coast decor runs towards beige. They call it sand, explain all the ways it connects the inside to the beach, but beige is fucking beige. There's no way of avoiding that. Sabbath never embraced the local motif. He renovated his suite in white and black, like he considered color an insult. White walls. White lights. White tiles. A dark couch and a deep, ink-colored coffee table. The sidebar lined with crystal decanters, and a big, fuck-off type television mounted on the wall. Sabbath's own private movie screen running a feed from the cameras downstairs, patrons throughout the casino engaged in the business of losing money.

Wesna dumped my pack, patted me down. She took her time about it, removed the contents from every pocket. There wasn't much. Spare change. A lighter. Three full clips for the SIG. They joined my other belongings on the coffee table. Wesna pointed towards the couch.

"Sit," she said.

I sat my ass down.

"Wait," she said.

I waited. Wesna emptied my pack and sifted through my laundry and second-hand paperbacks. Once satisfied there was nothing worth finding, she knocked on one of the big black doors leading into Sabbath's study. It cracked open, and she talked with the person on the far side. I couldn't pick up the specifics. I didn't need to. The door closed and Wesna fell in beside the couch, close enough to hurt me if I did something stupid.

Sabbath emerged ten minutes later—a short, neat man trailed by a bodyguard. The security was sleek and wide-shouldered, built to play front-row in the Rugby Sevens. Sabbath wore glasses, kept his graying hair cropped close to the scalp. He sat on the black couch opposite mine. Folded his arms. His white linen suit shone under the bright lights. Three hundred dollar sandals, his manicured toe nails on display.

He looked at Wesna. Looked at me. Studied all my shit, spread out over his coffee table. Sabbath lifted my copy of *Persuasion* from the pile. "I wouldn't have picked you as a reader, Murphy."

"That's because I wasn't, when you employed me." I kept my voice even. The sight of him flicking through the book made me irrationally angry, but anger was just going to get me in trouble. I took a deep breath, steadied my nerves. "Reading's a habit I accumulated along the way. Lots of long nights in my job, now."

"Lots of long nights," Sabbath repeated, thumbing through the dog-earned pages, checking out the points I'd marked. "So a few hours ago, I hear this rumor. Someone says Keith Murphy's returned, and he's chowing down at the Hard Rock on a burger and fries."

The twin pits of Sabbath's dark stare bore down on me. "Now, personally, I thought they were crazy," he said. "I told 'em Big Keith Murphy fucked off sixteen years back, and he sure as hell knows better than to come home. We all knew what would happen if Big Keith showed his face again, 'cause me and Danny Roark had ourselves a deal and it laid all that out. I told 'em in intimate, bloody detail how that deal was off if you ever stepped foot on the Coast. It made me a little warm, to imagine you might be dumb enough to break the agreement, you know? Just didn't think you'd do it."

Sabbath took a deep breath, tossed my book into the pile of clothes scattered across the coffee table. "The discovery that you're catching up on the classics, instead of getting bloated on junk food, does nothing to improve my mood."

"I did eat a burger, if that helps."

His eyes narrowed, fighting a smile. "That depends. How was it?"

"Okay," I said. "Too much cheese."

"Huh." He lost interest in my pile of stuff, turned toward Wesna. "You got his gun?"

She produced the SIG, handed it over. Sabbath freed the clip, held it to his nose to catch the familiar scent. His expression soured. "Holy water?"

"Soaked the top halves for a good four hours," I said. "Found a Pastor down in Byron with an erstwhile belief in the almighty. A pit-stop on the way through and a generous donation scored me a decent supply."

"Impressive." Sabbath slid the clip in place, held the pistol at arm's length. "But ultimately non-lethal to one of my kind."

He put the SIG on the coffee table, close enough for me to reach if I was sufficiently stupid to lunge for it. My younger self would have jumped for the gun. I wasn't that guy anymore. "Maybe painful's all I was looking for in a weapon."

"That," Sabbath said, "would be a very poor choice on your part." He dropped his weight back into the couch, tapping his index fingers together. Fixed the hollow eyes in my direction. "You represent something of a conundrum, Mister Murphy."

"Not sure why." I glanced down at the table, all my stuff strewn across it. "You've got me dead to rights, no point in hiding anything. I can strip down to my skivvies if you want to do a thorough search."

Sabbath's frown grew deeper. "Don't pretend to be an idiot, Murphy. I know you're not."

"No?"

"We've caught wind of your activities in Adelaide," Sabbath said. "There're rumors about an unfortunate incident, and the demise of a senior necromancer. Messy bit of business, that. Terrible consequences."

"Angry cultists," I said. "An irate soul. Some kind of death curse, the way I understand it."

I feigned confidence, forced myself to keep breathing. Watched Sabbath wrestle with two sets of instincts. The first set told him to rip me apart, just like he'd promised to when I walked away. The second set warned him I could be useful, even if I came with baggage. Desperation made people pliable, and Sabbath loved working with the desperate.

"That's a lot of trouble." His lip curled around the words.

"Not so much," I said. "We've got it under control and all."

"We?"

"Roark and me." I leant forward. "You remember Danny, right?"

That earned a low, glottal snarl from Sabbath. Yeah, he remembered Danny Roark. For a moment I caught a hint of fire in the shadowy depths of his eyes. He beat it down. Played it calm. A demon without a grudge. "Where is Mister Roark?" he purred. "I'd welcome the chance to reacquaint myself."

I flashed a grin and held steady. "Like you said, I'm not an idiot."

Sabbath nodded. He liked that. Always enjoyed a game. "I could have Wesna break fingers until you talked."

"All that gets us is ten broken digits and another round of this same conversation."

"Maybe," Sabbath said. "But then we get creative." He looked up at Wesna, a smile playing at his lips. "It's been a long time since we broke someone. I fear our technique could be rusty."

"Okay," I said. "We can go that direction, and we both know I'm only human. You'll get the screaming and the begging. Easy as. But Roark? It can't get you any closer to him. We ain't stupid, Sabbath. We took precautions. I'm here. He's in the wind, and I don't know where. Won't even call until after this meeting's done."

Another nod. "Smart," Sabbath said.

"It's not like I came back on a whim." I glanced at Wesna. She had the .32 out, discretely tucked under her free hand. Not pointed at me, but waiting for the order. I returned my focus to Sabbath, and his smile bloomed into life.

"Tell me about Adelaide."

"Big city. Middle of the desert. Does a good meat pie."

"Cut the shit," Sabbath said. "I only have so much patience. I've allowed you to live this long because I may have use for you, and that just weighs out against the pleasure I'd gain from having you ripped apart." He leaned forward, fixed me with a horrible stare. "Convince me you're actually useful, Keith. You'll only get one shot at it."

"Fine," I said. "Let's cut the shit. You know about Adelaide, and you've already guessed why I'm here. I need to lie low. I pissed off a cult. Turns out, with the Ravens, it's not a case of cutting off the head and leaving the body to die. And because Adelaide's in play, you've heard about the rest. All the jobs that went right. All the entities we eliminated, me and Roark. That's what I'm offering."

Sabbath sat back, did the thing where he tapped his fingertips together once more. "I've got my own approach to taking care of problems."

"I've been part of your crew. They're blunt instruments."

Sabbath shrugged. "They get the job done."

"Then why am I sitting here? Wesna could have left me to bleed out in the Hard Rock bathrooms."

I watched Sabbath sort through the ways he could play this, examining each half-truth and setting it aside. He enjoyed the game, always did. Bluff and counter. Looking for tells. He wouldn't go all-in on my offer, not without knowing more, but he'd pay to see my cards. That'd buy him time to puzzle out my habits. That bought me time to figure out the next step.

"All right," he said. "I've got some local nuisances I'd like eliminated, and your status as someone outside my organization makes you a somewhat useful tool. I could trade you a period of tolerance inside the city limits, in exchange for your specialized talents."

"How long are you offering?"

"I'm thinking six months."

I thought about Adelaide. The mess we'd made down there. "I may need longer. A year at least."

"Then we'll find ourselves back here, negotiating a second extension," Sabbath said. "You get six months, and in return I deploy you to take care of three problems. I give you the targets and time-frames, and they die in the timeline I nominate. That earns you a single promise: none of mine are coming after you until the agreed period is up. I've got no interest in defending you, Murphy."

"And I'm not looking for a bodyguard." I stood up, glanced down at my gear sprawled across the coffee table. "You know there's a limit on who I'll hunt."

"Even with your life on the line?"

"It's not much of a life right now. I'd hate to trade it for an innocent's."

"Well, then. Best I commit to picking my targets with care." Sabbath spread his fingers. "Relax, Murphy. I won't ask you to shoot any mortals that don't have it coming."

"By whose standards? Yours or mine?"

"Yours, I suppose." Sabbath grinned. "If that's what it takes to get this done."

I nodded, pointed at my gear. "I assume one of yours will bring all that down to the bar, once you've contented yourself that none of it is interesting?"

Sabbath shrugged again, his attention on the TV screen. He got what he wanted. Now the conversation was over. Wesna put a hand on my shoulder, guided me towards the door. The hall was cool and dry, courtesy of the air conditioning. "Twenty minutes," she said. "Assuming we discover nothing."

I caught the elevator down to the ground floor, confident they wouldn't find anything to derail this deal.

After all, the only thing worth finding was nestled in the pit of my stomach, burning like a hot coal.

I nursed a bourbon in the Atrium bar, waiting for one of Sabbath's flunkies to return my bag. I figured they'd be awhile, going through everything with a fine-toothed comb. Keep eyes on me to see if I sweated the search, trying to gauge the odds I'd brought the soul cage across the city limits.

I killed the time by speculating Sabbath's next move, when he turned up nothing. Smart money suggested they'd picked up intel about Wotan, and Sabbath would figure I'd hidden the cage before surfacing in the Hard Rock. That made our deal attractive, gave Sabbath a few weeks to observe and suss out my play. One demon might suggest cutting me open, doing a messy search of my innards, but odds were Sabbath regarded that as a last-resort. For one thing, it meant they were out of options if my innards turned up nothing.

For another, Sabbath wanted me to suffer, even if he played things professional for now. Death let me off the hook, limited him to a single punishment. Alive, he could torture me for weeks and months.

Their second assumption would involve Danny Roark holding the soul cage, and the possibility of using me as leverage would appeal to Sabbath. That too would keep me breathing for a stretch, albeit uncomfortably.

I finished my bourbon. Ordered another. Wesna showed up halfway through the drink, handed me the backpack. "Your six months starts now," she said. "I call you in a week or two, and we discuss the first job. You and me, not you and him. Sabbath's preference involves not seeing you for a while, lest he give into temptation."

"The feeling's more than mutual." I sipped my bourbon. Rolled it across my tongue. "Where we meeting?"

"Wherever you end up staying." Wesna produced a cell phone, tucked it into my pocket. "Burner. Untraceable. My number's the only one in there."

I put down my glass. Picked up my pack. "Pleasure doing business with you, then."

She gave me a hard look. "Screw up once, and he'll have you. He's not fucking around with that. Whatever shit you're running from, don't let it spoil this deal."

I slung my backpack over my shoulder. "You worry too much, Wes."

"Like hell I do." Wesna flagged the bartender, ordered a scotch of her own. "You planning on seeing Nora?"

I'd spent sixteen years working with Danny Roark, learning how to keep my emotions in check when talking to demons. I'd gotten pretty good at it, but her name brought all the memories back. When I abandoned the Gold Coast, Nora Otto was the only thing I gave a damn about leaving behind. I hooked my pack over my shoulder. "Nah, I don't think that's wise."

"You know she searched for you, right? Tracked me down and started asking questions about work."

"And you told her?"

"Just what you'd want me to tell her: that you were an asshole and no one could say where you ran off too." Wesna attempted to hide the grin behind her bourbon.

"Good call."

"She didn't take it well."

"Taking things well wasn't her style."

"You should go see her," Wesna said.

"It's not a good idea." I looked into my empty glass, contemplated having another. Decided against it. Ancient history is better left in the past and getting drunk in front of Wesna would give her a chance to fish.

Plus, the soul cage in my gut sat there like a stone, an insistent reminder to keep on the move until I'd reached somewhere safe.

"Listen," I said, "I'm off. You get a job, you call me. Otherwise, just leave me alone."

I stopped off at the payphones by the lift, dropped coins into the slot and dialed the number Roark had me memorize in case we ever found ourselves separated and in deep shit. It rang a half-dozen times before a brisk, female voice answered: "So, you're still alive, then?"

"For the moment," I told her. "We've come to an accord."

"And now you need a ride?"

"I do."

"I'm down in the car park," the voice said. "Third floor. Row J. I'll keep an eye out."

SAFETY IS A STATE OF MIND

I found her parked on the far end of the lot, near the exit that directed traffic towards the shopping mall across the road. Holly Langford perched on the bonnet of a less-than-pristine HR Holden. The car looked out of place, the boxy sixties design mocked by the rows of sleek, modern hatchbacks and four-wheel drives. Langford flicked her cigarette over the concrete rail, slid off the HR and scuffed her Docs against the floor. "Well, shit, you're alive" she said. "I take it negotiations turned out better than expected?"

"They went okay."

"It thrills me when you say that, mate. Inspires all kinds of fucking confidence."

I didn't blame Langford for being pissed. She'd known me for twenty-four hours, ever since I'd called her and invoked Roark's name. She owed Roark some favors, from his life before we met. Like most sorcerers, she believed in paying back her debts.

I clambered into the passenger side of the HR. Langford slid in behind the wheel and lit a second cigarette, lips pressed tight to hold it in place. The big car suited her. She was six-three. Skinny. Looked about forty-five, but I didn't have any faith in my estimate because the piercings through her nose, lip, and eyebrows made it easy to low-ball her age. So did the dreadlocks that hung past her shoulders.

Thick, knotted tattoos covered her forearms; Celtic work,. Designed to obscure the ink with actual power. She reversed out, put the car in gear, and headed into the outside world. "So what great and terrible hijinks hide behind your 'okay,' then?"

I pressed my head against the window, watched the once-familiar landscape slip past. "Who says there's hijinks?"

"Bitter experience," she said. "I know Danny Roark. I've seen the kind of shit that nips at his heels."

The cigarette smoke burnt itself into my nostrils, thick and pungent. I coughed into my fist, but she didn't take the hint. Just stared at the road, eyes bright and focused. "Well?"

"Three jobs. A six-month stay of execution."

"Jesus."

"It's not that bad," I said. "No worse than I expected going in."

"Spoken like a stupid git who's spent too long around Danny." We hit the highway, and she pressed her foot against the accelerator. Eight cylinders of analog engine roared beneath the hood. Langford took care of the vehicle, lavished more attention on the working parts than the battered, powder-blue shell.

"When this is over," Langford said, "I'm making myself a voodoo doll and spending some quality time giving you a headache." Her thin, tattooed arms hauled the wheel as we pulled into the slow-moving traffic. "You sure you don't know where Roark is?"

"West, somewhere. That's all he gave me."

She held the cigarette between two fingers and grunted her dissatisfaction with my answer. I closed my eyes and kept my mouth shut, listened to the rhythm of Surfers receding into the distance. We were heading south, away from the tourist heart of the Coast, leaving behind the casino and the shopping mall and the rows of pristine towers designed for temporary occupation. I'd been running on fumes since Adelaide. I wanted a place to shower, a hamburger, and safe, private spot to shit out the 9mm soul cage lodged in my intestines.

Langford fired the stereo, found an old punk song on the FM dial. "So tell me about the fuck-up," she said. "I mean, I asked around, while you were meeting with your demon friends, but…"

I yawned and covered my mouth with a fist. "It's not much of a story."

"That's Roark for 'I don't want to talk about it.'"

"Yeah, I guess it is."

"He wouldn't get away with it either," she said. "Not with what you're asking. If we're hunting the local denizens of the Gloom, I'd kinda like to know you aren't a complete incompetent."

The bitterness in my laugh surprised me. "Okay. That's fair enough."

"So?"

I watched the landscape roll by, stitching unfamiliar landmarks over bits of memory. Every block, as we rolled past the cross-street, I glimpsed the beach framed between the rows of buildings. "I wanted to get out of the game, and he coaxed me into one last job. Roark picked us a target in Adelaide," I said. "Some necromancer type, head of his own cult. It's serial killer central down there, so he had plenty of juice to work with. Enough to build up a serious following."

"And?"

"And we underestimated his power. We got the guy, no trouble. Siphoned his spirit into a soul trap, so they couldn't bring him back. It should have been a clean, easy job. In and out. Next thing I know, Roark's telling me to run and put in a call to you. Says he'll be heading out west to draw them off."

"Shit." Langford frowned at the steering wheel. "You fuckers took on Wotan?"

"We did."

She swore again, eased the car around the long curve at Burleigh Heads. For a moment the rows of high-rises gave way to an open expanse of park, stretching towards the pristine water. Another turn and they disappeared behind the rise of Burleigh Hill.

"You know of him?"

"Who?"

"The hit," I said. "This Wotan asshole."

"Mostly by reputation." Langford took a drag on her cigarette, stubbed it into the ashtray. "Wotan's venerable enough to remember the Gloom before it became corrupted. Rumor is he worshipped the Old Gods, cut deals with the Giants that sleep in the bottom of the darkness. I mean, shit, there were folks who claimed Michael Wotan was immortal." She shook her head, dreadlocks brushing against her shoulders. "Why in fuck would you try to take him down?"

I shrugged. "Roark said it was necessary, and it was our last. Figured we'd go out big."

"It didn't occur to you he might be wrong?"

The punk song ended and Langford thumbed the stereo band, searched until she found the classic rock station. Led Zeppelin blared through the car, loud enough to make my ears bleed. I contemplated a request to drop the volume, and decided against it. I needed Langford on my side. That wasn't a feeling I liked.

We hit the end of "Immigrant Song" and she dialed the racket back a few levels. "So who's got the soul cage, you or him?"

She said it quietly, like the possible answers frightened her. I kept my face still, gave away nothing. "Roark ever strike you as the kid of guy who'd let me carry the football? The old man trusts me, more or less, but I just pull the trigger. I don't mess with anything beyond the very basics."

Langford nodded. Adjusted her grip, thin fingers fluttering against the wheel. "This needs to be clear up front," she said, "I'll get you to the safe house. I'll help with your deal, because I owe Danny that much. Once that debts repaid, I'm out. You understand me?"

"Yeah," I said. "I get it."

"This part, though, I want crystal," Langford said. "Anything associated with Michael Wotan is asking for all kinds of trouble. If you're lying about the cage, if his soul or his followers show up, I'll abandon your ass so fast you'll wonder if I ever existed."

She folded down the visor, lifted another cigarette out of the pack she stored there. "I never bought in to Danny's crusade. I don't owe him enough to get started now."

Langford set me up in a safe house the beach side of Currumbin Hill. She let me in, handed over the keys, then loitered in the kitchen while I checked the place out. Two stories and narrow, like they'd built a three-story apartment in an oversized fence picket hammered into the steep slope. The price tag on the property probably breached a million—a luxury holiday spot positioned to catch the sunlight and the breeze, hidden behind a high wall to block the view for the rest of the street.

I dumped my gear in a bedroom with a king-sized bed that doubled as modern art. Too tired to care about how nice the place was. I'd been awake too long and the contents of my stomach weighed like a swallowed sandbag.

Still, under different circumstances it would have been an incredible view. The downhill slope had been declared a nature preserve, which meant everything below me was trees and scrub. A melodic chortle of magpies launched into their morning chorus, their warble mingling with the steady pulse of the waves. The ocean stretched out, uninterrupted, to the horizon. If it wasn't for the resort tucked at the base of the hill, I could have convinced myself it was some place pleasant.

I stood at the window for a stretch. Migrated to the bathroom after that, where I spent futile minutes trying to combat the oxycodone and antacid I'd used to keep me blocked. I curled up on the toilet, cramped to hell. Tried not to ponder what would happen if my stomach acid breached the condom tied around the bullet with Wotan's soul inside.

Langford was making coffee when I finally I emerged. Plunger, not instant. The mugs were pristine and white. "Will it do?" she said.

"I'm accustomed to cheaper."

"I'll bet you're used to squalor." Langford handed me a steaming mug, nursed the other one in her left hand. "I've worked with Danny a time or two. The man lives for dingy hotel rooms."

"He's not that bad," I said.

"Say that after you've slept on a mattress that's never known the touch of bed-bugs." Langford settled into the leather couch, watched me pace the room. "It belongs to some friends of mine, currently overseas," she said. "The neighbors are seasonal—no one around this time of year—and everybody's used to visitors dropping in and out. I'm assuming you know enough to set wards?"

"I'll get by." I tried perching on the windowsill. Decided against it when my bowels disagreed.

"Try to keep it neat and discrete, then." Langford frowned, distracted herself with the coffee. "No blood on the carpet, and try not to trash the place defending yourself, if someone tracks you here."

"They won't," I said, trying to make it sound like I believed that was true.

"Please," Langford said. "I've worked with Danny."

"But I'm not Roark."

"That isn't exactly a comfort." She finished her coffee, dropped the mug in the sink. "Once I leave this place, I'm forgetting your ass is here," she said. "We meet out in the city. Navigate your own way there and cover your own damn butt."

I made positive noises, like I understood where she was coming from. Hell, who knows? Maybe I actually did, somewhere down below the fear and the anger that came with being home again. I was back on the Gold Coast. I was working for Sabbath again. One fuck-up on a job down in Adelaide and I'd wiped away everything good about my life, reverted to the same piece-of-shit I used to be when I was twenty and scared of the things I saw in the shadows.

But Langford wasn't Roark, and trust didn't come easy for either of us. I drained my coffee. Looked her in the eye. "I'll take care of the place," I said. "Sixteen years, I handled my end, no problems. Adelaide's the only time we fucked up."

"You wanted out for a reason."

"And it had nothing to do with my abilities."

Langford considered the validity of my statement, nodded her acceptance. She gathered her keys and stood up. Gave me a final once-over. "When do we hear about the first target?"

"Wesna calls me. I call you," I said. "My guess? Seven days or so. He'll want to think about how to torture me with it."

"I'll see you in a week then," Langford said. "You've got my number."

I sat by the front door, watched her leave. Waited a good hour before I hiked through the scrub to the bottom of the hill, then caught a bus to Palm Beach and the open-all-night chemist. The girl behind the counter offered me a friendly smile.

"How can I help ya?" she said.

"Laxatives," I said. "Strongest you've got."

THE FIRST HIT

My predictions regarding the first hit were out by three days. Wesna rang me mid-way through my evening workout, invited me to dinner at the twenty-four-hour McDonald's up on Burleigh Beach. She laid out the client's details over cheeseburgers and vanilla shakes, slipping me an envelope with a trio of grainy photographs printed from a cell phone.

"Target's name us Eddie Darius," she said. "He's a small-time warlock operating out of the parks in Southport, recruiting kids from the homeless that camp-out on the foreshore. We don't know who he worships, but they're not a major player. You want to keep the photos?"

I shook my head. The photographs weren't great quality, but they gave me a decent idea what to look for: short and thin, unwashed hair draped across his sallow features. Flannel shirts habitually tied around his waist. Army surplus backpack slung over his shoulder. A lot of the shots featured Darius on the foreshore, hanging out with guys whose wide-eyed expressions said they'd seen too much. I kept flipping through the images, found the one I wanted: a close-up on his right arm, covered in dark ink.

"His tat's look Sumerian." I flipped the photograph

around, pointed out a marking of a multi-headed snake. "Tiamat, maybe? She's old, though. Where in hell does a punk his age find a ritual for contacting an entity that ancient?"

Wesna rolled her eyes. "Who he worships doesn't concern us. It's how that's become a problem."

I placed the photographs back into their envelope. Pushed it across the table. "Sloppy?"

"To put it mildly," she said. "His disposal techniques leave something to be desired. Sabbath's agreement with the mortal powers-that-be..."

Wesna didn't bother finishing that. There wasn't any need. The Other thrived on the Gold Coast because they lived beneath the radar, taking advantage of the transient population where no one stuck around for all that long. The local cops adopted a professional disinterest when people disappeared. They started paying attention when the bodies showed up in significant numbers.

"Okay," I said. "Give me a time frame."

Wesna's lip curled. "Two weeks."

"For surveillance?"

"For the whole thing," she said. "He's built his rituals around the full moon. The cops haven't identified the pattern, but they will. They're on the verge of saying serial killer, once they do. We'd prefer they don't raise suspicions about the occult being involved."

"The usual timeline is four."

"Then call it a rush job," Wesna said. "Sabbath assumes you're up to it, given your years of experience."

"Come on, Wes."

"No. I gave you the opportunity to run, and you elected to make a deal instead." She folded her arms, stared me down. "There's a part of me that would still regret pulling you apart. It would take the fun out of things, if Sabbath ordered it."

I waited for her to smile, shrug that off as a joke. Realized, when she stood, there wasn't that much humor left inside her. Wesna disappeared into the rainy night. Off to do whatever shadowy tasks Sabbath needed her doing, up to and including dissecting me for crossing him.

It isn't easy, killing a warlock. Even a minor, bottom-of-the-totem-pole motherfucker as useless as Eddie Darius. You need to be certain who they're worshipping, what kind of defenses they've set up to cover their butt, and how they'll respond to being killed. Otherwise you risk being haunted by the warlock's ghost, or you trigger some convoluted death curse against the hand that gunned them down. You sure as hell don't want to be on the run, hiding a soul cage beneath the floorboards in your safe house, hoping the wards will hold if the cultists ever track you down.

I called into Langford, laid out the job. She bitched about the timeframes, but she took up the lion's share of the passive's role, scouting the target and looking for the routines and the little daily rituals we could exploit to take him down. Occasionally I'd spell her, taking a shift in the van we used to follow Darius around, giving her time to go do some research or catch a few hours sleep.

It wasn't ideal. It never is.

The two key parts of the passive's job are scouting routines and identifying occult defenses. Fortunately, Darius proved to be a creature of consistent habits. He woke late and haunted the two-story Antique and Collector's Bookstore on Scarborough Street. Langford theorized the A&C was ground zero for his interest in magic and the Gloom. Despite its name, the bookshop stocked the same collection of cheap paperbacks every other store on the Gold Coast carried: years of accumulated holiday reads left behind by tourists. Its antiquarian section catered to a select clientele, and the owner kept his day staff away from those who sought more than first-edition copies of *Moby Dick* and *Great Expectations*.

Darius spent his afternoons down by the Broadwater, in the park beneath the Sundale bridge. A gathering place for the local homeless kids, motley clans of runaway teens, assorted junkies, and unhinged folks turfed out of the public hospital. I'd camped there myself, in my teenage years, right about the point the government closed the rehab clinic attached to Southport Hospital. The closure had been first steps of an urban renewal that never took hold.

Darius had a flat, but he dressed down to deal heroin and spend hours listening to the ramblings of the craziest of the burnouts. It wasn't unusual. It's a phase most aspiring sorcerers go through, not long after they realize the world contains more secrets than they suspected. A lot of them theorize that contact with the Gloom is the source of many off-kilter rants heard on street corners. It's rare that they're right, and even on the occasions they are, there are more lucid sources than those poor folks broken by unprotected exposure to the Gloom.

We spent the two weeks on surveillance, waiting for the full moon and the night of his rituals. I squatted in the passenger seat of the van, doing the final watch. Langford sat behind the wheel, working her way through a pack of Winfield Blues.

"I don't know about you," she said, "but I kinda hate this guy." She took a long drag on her cigarette, eyes never leaving the park. Darius was talking to a sixteen-year-old girl, a blonde with matted hair and a grubby blue Quicksilver jacket. "Third time our friend has talked to her in a week. Dollars to donuts, that's who he's hoping to take home for a sacrifice."

"Could be courting a new customer."

"Please."

I peered at him through binoculars. "She represents a break in his pattern?"

"Big enough," Langford said. "Ordinarily, by this point, he'd have stopped by, sold, and moved on, burned through his spiel about the glory of whatever pissant entity he's lucked into worshipping. Then he'd head further down the bank, where he can listen to Old Mate rant a bit, see if he can learn anything."

She pointed to an elderly bloke who camped out on a patch of grass by the swings. Darius kept glancing his way, but didn't move over. His attention was on the girl, laying it on thick.

"You got a handle on his defenses?"

"Sure." Langford finished her cigarette and unearthed the pack to forage for another. "They're basic wards. You could break them, if you put your mind to it. You got a plan to take him out?"

"Figured I'd make all his dreams come true."

Langford lit up. "Risky choice."

"It's neat. It takes care of the body, and Sabbath wants these looking accidental."

Langford sucked on her cigarette, free hand toying with the end of a dreadlock. "Any other job, I'd tell ya we need more lead-in," she said, "but this guy's a lightweight. I'll give you ten bucks on him shitting himself the moment a portal opens."

"You reckon we can pull it off?"

"So long as you hold up your part," she said. "Keep watch on our friend here, and I'll go set things up."

Eddie Darius rented an apartment in an old motel. The sign out front identified the place as Palm Cove, but it hadn't been lit up in over a decade and there were no signs of palms or coves anywhere on the property.

The layout offered several good entry points: two stairwells leading up to the second floor landing shared by three separate units, a narrow balcony on the far side accessible from a badly positioned picnic table. No working lights in the rear stairwell, no defenses over the external parts of the block. Darius focused security on his apartment, basic wards. Langford was right: I could tear them down myself.

"Dark stairwell's your way in," Langford said. "Nobody's used it after sunset for two straight weeks, so it'll give you somewhere to hang if we cloak your presence. Wait for this fuckhead to leave, and you can stroll past his protections with no trouble."

"He won't sense me?"

"If the timetables right, he's going to be focused on the girl he's courting for the next sacrifice. Small-time fuckers already convinced himself he's damned unstoppable. No way Darius is expecting anyone to jump him."

"Might not wait for him inside, then," I said. "Better to keep the sacrifice out of the apartment."

Langford shrugged. "Your call, trigger."

I settled in around nine o'clock, waited a few hours for Eddie Darius to return. It's the hardest part of the job, sometimes. The loiter, doing nothing, making sure you're not spotted. I busied myself with a minor charm Roark taught me, one that encouraged people not to see you if they glanced your way. It gave me something to concentrate on, instead of pacing the narrow stairwell. The tether marks on my forearms hummed, drawing power fro the Gloom.

Eddie Darius reappeared at 11:05, homeless girl on his arm. Her features matched the sacrifice he'd been grooming in Langford's surveillance photographs: blonde and street-skin thin, big eyes and a wide mouth. Her instincts proved stronger than his, clocking my presence as the target fumbled with the keys. She backed away when I emerged from the shadows.

The target kept talking to her, not really paying attention. I got halfway along the landing, produced the SIG and held it against my side in a calm, steady grip. "Mister Darius?"

He startled at his name and glanced down at the pistol. Put two-and-two together real quick, for a moron like him. "Oh man," he said.

I gestured to the girl. "Miss, you may wish to leave now.".

Darius whipped his head around just in time to see her retreating. He turned back to me, eyes narrowed. Moving past the shock, Darius stumbled into the phase where he was trying to calculate what my presence meant.

He glanced down at the SIG again. The part he couldn't work out. Most newly-minted users of the Gloom expect their enemies to fight magic with magic.

"Let's go inside," I said. "We can talk in private."

For a moment I saw hope rise within him, but it died when he realized Langford had disabled all his wards. Darius stepped into the kitchen. I followed him, closed the door behind me. There wasn't much to his apartment. Shitty kitchenette. Shitty lounge room. Where most people had a couch and TV, he had a big square of granite, a ritual circle carved into the dark stone. He'd devoted a lot of effort to the boundary of his summoning space. Four feet wide, candles at even points, dried blood in the center. The knife looked like a prop from a B-Grade movie. Amateur shit, all of it. That didn't surprise me. The Gloom responded to concentrated emotions and beliefs. Newly minted warlocks and sorcerers treat the trappings of their rituals like training wheels, unable to shape the Gloom without all the horror-film aesthetics to bolster their confidence.

Darius edged close to the granite. Tried to hide the way he glanced down at the knife.

"Don't," I said.

He stopped. Waited for my next move. I still had the SIG pointed at the floor, held in a steady, two-handed grip. Darius whet his lips, mind whirring. "Listen, man," he said. "I don't have nothing worth stealing, right?"

"Bull."

"Come on, dude. Look at this place. What in hell do you think you're getting?"

"Everyone's got something valuable enough to take." I lifted the SIG to cover him and whispered one of the first spells Roark ever taught me. The twelve candles spread around the circle caught alight in unison. "Don't shit me, Darius. I know what you do here."

Darius stepped away from the altar, an easy smile forming on his lips. "Well," he said, "I suppose that changes things, somewhat." He dipped his knee, approximating a bow without ever lowering his hands. "Welcome, brother, to my san——"

"If you say sanctum, I'll shoot you where you stand," I said. "It's a goddamn lounge room, kid. Invest in candles and blood all you want—this shithole will never be a sanctum."

Darius closed his mouth. Gnawed his lower lip. "If you knew what I did here—"

"I know," I said. "I can even guess exactly what good you've done with it. Week after week, trying to open a portal. Killing those kids, carting off the bodies. Lazy work. Unimpressive."

"Lazy?" He couldn't quite process that. I almost felt sorry for him. The kid had learned the basics from someone, figured out enough to put together a ritual circle and contact one of the entities that lay in the deep Gloom. With tutelage, he could have been a solid sorcerer. As it is, he remained a goddamn menace to those around him.

"Lazy," I said. "All that blood. All these fucking props. You've got no idea how any of this shit works, do you?"

"I've learned enough," Darius said.

"Yeah?" I slipped the SIG into my waistband, picked up the gaudy knife he used in his rituals. "Well Darius, I guess it's your lucky day. I don't want to hurt you—not my job. I'm just here to stop you from making another mess. So you show me how much you know, and if you can get through this without dumping a corpse in the river, I might not have to put a bullet in your skull."

Darius whet his lips again, glanced down at the circle. "But—"

He cut himself off the moment I looked up. "Yeah? But?"

"I need the girl," Darius said. "A sacrifice. Mother Tiamat demands it, before she'll grant me—"

I grabbed his wrist and sliced the gaudy knife across his palm. For all his faults, Darius kept the blade sharp. Blood pooled, welling out of the wound. He swore three or four times, but my tight grip held the drips over the carved granite and charged up the ritual circle. His breath caught as Darius felt the first surge of power.

"Blood's easy," I said. "Make contact to bolster it."

Darius slapping his palm down on the circle. Left a long, crimson smear over the older, darker stains. "And now there's a sacrifice. Lesson one: a thimble's as good as a bucket, when you're dealing with the Other."

Darius nursed his bleeding hand, pressing it against his t-shirt. It didn't stop the injury from leaking, but it left an impressive stain. I cast the knife aside, pulled the SIG again. That got his attention. "Don't focus on the pain. It's only temporary."

"I don't..." Darius fumbled over the words. Fear robbed him of the ability to finish the sentence.

"Kneel," I said.

He knelt.

I stepped back from the granite, gave him plenty of room. "Go ahead. Introduce me to your goddess."

"I can't—"

"Yes, you can," I said. "Deep breaths, concentrate on what you want to achieve."

He wanted to object, but I raised the SIG and trained it in his direction. The gun seemed to give him focus, clarify the world so he understood the two options available to him. He knelt by the altar, dripped blood from his palm over the circle. Slowly, quietly, he started to chant. I didn't recognize the words, but I recognized the rhythm.

Nervously, desperately, Eddie Darius reached out to the far side of the Gloom and tried to contact his goddess. I held my breath, waited, let the unsteady cadence of his voice fill the room. The temperature dropped as thickening shadows spread through the circle, seeping free like a stream of dark tears.

Darius hesitated, startled by the unexpected result. "Don't," I said. "Keep going."

He swallowed and resumed the chant, eyes wide. The darkness congealed, thickened. Became something more as it touched the Gloom. Eddie Darius faltered, unable to look away from its depths.

A tenebrous tentacle stretched from the Gloom and caressed the side of his face. More of them reached along the edges of the circle, testing for restraints, found none. Darius retreated, hit the wall. He kept trying to go back, like he hadn't noticed he'd run out of room.

"What the fuck?" Darius whispered, over and over. "What the fucking fuck?"

Part of me pitied him.

I put a bullet in right leg, just above the knee. Eddie Darius shrieked, what little self-control he still had shattering in that instant. The tentacles shivered, feeding on his shock and the sudden rush of agony. As one, they reached for Darius and wrapped around him, dragging him into the circle with cold, implacable purpose. Eddie Darius screamed for a few short seconds, then he disappeared into the depths, drawn into the place on the far side of the Gloom.

I kept my breathing steady, did my best to feel nothing at all. Waited a full minute before I risked moving. The older entities of the Gloom, little-worshipped and mostly forgotten, were easy to placate. Offer them a brush against our plane of existence and a terrified victim to snack on, and they're content to lapse back to their dormant state unless you keep goading them into consciousness. Whatever goddess Darius worshiped probably didn't even wake out of her slumber after she took him.

But you never assume that, not once there's an open portal in play. I let the darkness thin in the center of the circle, made sure there was nothing but granite underneath it. Then I collected the shell from the single shot, slipped it into the pocket of my jeans, and locked the front door behind me.

DOWNTIME

I spent a few weeks falling into a routine, despite my best intentions.

The safe house's design encouraged repetition. The tall, thin rooms encouraged horizontal living. All the furniture pressed against the western side of the building, leaving a clear path along the windows that faced out towards the horizon. They weren't even windows: the east-facing wall comprised glass panels, capitalizing on the downhill view of gumtrees, beach, and sea. Visually spectacular but damned inconvenient. When daylight broke, the sun beamed into the bedroom and slapped me awake. Ensured a regular wake-up and made it damn near impossible to get back to sleep.

In theory, I was okay with that. The hours spent unconscious are the enemy when you're hiding out. You're at your most vulnerable, forced to trust your defenses will keep you secure. In practice, I minimized slumber in the worst possible way, devoted my mornings to the free-weights I found in the bedroom wardrobe. Gave my afternoons over to taking care of the place, staying tidy. Double checking my protections and keeping an eye out for trouble. Cleaned the SIG on the glass-topped coffee table, like a ritual.

Once a week I'd pull out the small wooden box I stashed beneath the floorboards under the bed. I lifted the defenses and flipped the lid, checked the bullet with Michael Wotan's soul sat exactly where it was meant to be. Afterwards, I closed everything and reinforced the wards. Slipped the whole deal back under, tucked into my go bag, and slid the floorboards back into place.

I ordered in groceries from the nearest supermarket, alternating the hour and day of each delivery to avoid establishing a pattern. One smart thing, at least. In the evenings I put the television on for the noise. That ended around ten o'clock, when anything worth watching was over-and-done with. Most nights, I'd listen to the waves. Re-read *Persuasion* for the second or third time. Killed the days while I waited for Roark to call and end our exile.

It didn't help. Not really. The part of the job where you sit tight and wait ground my nerves to paste, left me feeling unsettled and ready to hit something. Staying in one place wasn't in my nature, not anymore. Sixteen years I'd worked jobs with Roark, drifting from city to city. We'd put down demons, fey, and sorcerers. We'd done the work that needed doing. Routine killed every target we hunted, before Roark first started his rituals and I first loaded a gun. Routine gave us the tools to pick apart their defenses.

Everybody developed routines, and smart killers hijacked them. All they required time, patience, and a rock-solid conviction the effort involved was worth the rewards.

I met Wesna in the McDonald's up at Burleigh Heads, discussed the details in a quiet booth in the restaurant's corner. She slid the envelope across the table, gave me a one month timeframe before the target needed to die. She watched my face, smirking, hoping for a reaction. I kept my cool, nodded. Told her it wouldn't be a problem.

I put a few blocks between us before I started swearing. Called Langford from a payphone down by Burleigh Beach, organized to meet with her an hour later.

The park wasn't a bad place to wait. Unlike most of the Coast's beachside parks, Burleigh deserved the name: a broad, green expanse that ended at the dunes, lots of tall pines that sheltered flocks of lorikeets in the afternoon. You could hit a cricket ball without fear of it going into the street. Families spent the day up there, during the holidays. The local feral tribes used Burleigh for drum circles and fire twirling every Saturday night. Surfers gave the shore a wide berth, preferring the break on the far side of the headlands.

I beat Langford there by twenty minutes, so I claimed a table for the wait. Langford showed up with two cups of coffee, slid one across as she sat down. It smelt good. Better than the cheap instant I resorted to at the safe house, and a huge improvement on the McCafé garbage I'd been drinking a few hours earlier.

"Thanks," I said.

Langford shrugged. "You sounded like you needed a decent caffeine hit."

Her smile dared me to deny that, but there wasn't much point. I sipped my coffee, stared at the dark horizon. "The next target is Nora Otto," I said. "She runs a club in Broadbeach, right under the Demon's noses."

"The Hell Bar," Langford said.

"You know the place?"

"I've done business on the premises, from time to time," she said.

"You ever met Otto?"

Langford shook her head.

"I have," I said. "We used to be friends."

"Friends, or *friends*."

"The second one."

Langford thought the implications over. Sipped her coffee.

"All right," she said. "You had to figure that was coming. You make a deal like yours with a demon who's holding a grudge..."

"Yeah," I said. "I figured he'd twist the knife."

"And?"

"Still a surprise," I said. "Nora didn't know about the Other, sixteen years back. Not sure how she ended up on Sabbath's radar."

"Ah," Langford said.

"Yeah, fucking 'ah'."

"And how does that change things?"

"That depends," I said. "How rotten is the bar?"

"It's bad." Langford flexed her thin fingers, adjusted her grip on the coffee mug. "Exactly the kind of club you and Roark go after. Mortals enticed in for the Other to prey upon, lots of people given a shit-load of money to keep the deaths hush-hush. No questions asked about what the Other do there, assuming they're discrete. Your demon friends wanting it taken down would surprise me, if it wasn't for the personal connection to the mistress of the house."

"I doubt her death will close things," I said. "Not for long, anyway."

Langford closed her eyes and pondered. "Otto would be a hard woman to replace," she said. "She's got a decade's experience handling the fey, always eager to deal with the minor players. Lots of people trust her to keep the club neutral; the moment that changes, they look for safer options. No one will depend on Sabbath to do that, even if they suspect that Otto's in his pocket."

"Is she?"

"Is she what?"

"Working for Sabbath?"

"Who knows?" Langford considered her coffee, raised the paper cup to her lips. "You operate in Broadbeach and you're doing some kind of arrangement with Sabbath and his crew.

How deep the deal goes is anyone's guess, but the illusion of minimal interference they've created is convincing."

She drank, stopped. Looked me in the eye. "If you're asking me if she deserves to die, that's something I can't tell you."

"Yeah." I sipped my coffee, not tasting it; tried to swallow too much hot liquid. It hurt as it went down, muscles contorting to keep my breathing clear. Langford thumped my back as I coughed and spluttered. I waved her off, wiped my mouth with my sleeve. "Shit," I said. "I remember why I hate it here."

Langford waited, letting me process. She finished her coffee, dumped the empty cups into a nearby bin. Sunlight bloodied the horizon.

"Well," she said, "it's your move, trigger. We using your connection as a tool to get close, or your excuse to walk away?"

"Neither," I said. "Business as usual. We start surveillance, pull together a plan. We've got thirty-days, and we either know it's worth doing by the end of that. If not, Sabbath's reneging on our deal and things get complicated."

"You think that's likely?"

"No," I said. "Sabbath's smarter than that. If he's got her on the list, he's confident she'd be a target if it weren't for our history. He swore that all his targets would deserve what they had coming."

"Yeah?" Langford snorted and rubbed her hands together, trying to generate some warmth. "By whose standards?"

"Mine," I said. "He was real damn careful about that one. Odds are, he's had this idea up his sleeve from the moment I arrived."

SURVEILANCE

There were ravens on the power-lines outside the Oasis complex. Two of them, sitting wing-to-wing, positioned so their dark eyes could scan the street. I crouched by tinted windowpane and Langford lay on her belly beside me, binoculars pressed to her face. I pointed out the corvids. "How long have they been there?"

Langford followed the line of my finger. "The birds?"

"Yeah."

"Few hours, maybe." The binoculars refocused on the front door of the Hell Bar.

"How many hours we talking?"

"Two? Three? I don't know." We were twenty days into surveillance, and my presence grated on her nerves. Langford wanted to ignore me, do her damn job, and bail out before things got crazy. Having me in the room increased the odds of something going wrong.

The ravens bothered me. "There's a big difference between two hours and three."

Langford abandoned the binoculars, flicked me an angry glare. "They're crows, trigger. More of them have been there, on and off."

"That just makes it worse."

"You're sure?"

"Roark spent a damn month ensuring I could recognize the difference, before we attempted the job down in Adelaide. Those guys are too big, and the curve happens towards the end of the beak," I said. "On a crow, you'd see it starting halfway down. Tail feathers would be the same length, less wedge, more fan."

She looked through the binoculars, then nodded, dreadlocks bobbing. "All right," she said. "I'll give you that. Doesn't mean they're trouble."

"Given the circumstances, I wouldn't rely on that," I said.

"Fine. I'll pay attention to 'em, if you're worried about it." Langford made a show of looking at her watch. "Twelve oh-nine. Your girl arrives in a couple of minutes, and we haven't got her process for bypassing the wards on the bar yet. You want to keep arguing about the damn birds?"

"I'm inclined to think about it," I said.

Langford snorted exasperated air into the still room. "And if they are familiars for whatever cult you're running from, how does it change your deal with Sabbath?"

"Well…"

Langford raised an eyebrow at me, but I had nowhere to go. She pressed her eyes against the binoculars again, attention focused on the bar.

I left her to it, went to the small kitchenette to make us some shitty instant coffee. Three weeks of surveillance on Nora Otto hadn't altered my feelings about the job. The residents heading into the Hell Bar weren't exactly the company I'd keep, but I'd be willing to bet Langford could name a dozen Other with similar reps and called them friend. Even Roark allied himself with dangerous Other, tolerating all kinds of creatures we'd have killed in other circumstances.

That's how it goes once you've seen Gloom. Nothing is ever really safe anymore.

"She's here," Langford said. "Usual park, down by the Surf Club."

I left the steaming mugs of coffee on the bench and walked back to the window. Watched as Nora Otto exited her beat-up Daihatsu and crossed the road. She moved with short, clipped steps, her gait limited by the leather skirt she wore to the bar like a uniform. Langford clicked her tongue at the choice. "Your girl has terrible fashion sense."

"Depends."

"Yeah? On what?"

"Whether the skirt's a statement," I said. "A fuck you to the creatures of the night, who naturally expect every mortal to run."

"If that's the case, she'd pair it with heels," Langford said. "Not steel-toed Docs."

The part of me that still thought with a teenager's hormones wanted to make a counter-argument. People noticed Nora Otto when she walked, and it wasn't just the short hemline that snared attention. She paired the leather skirt with a professional jacket, midway between corporate and punk. In the sixteen years I'd been away, she'd grown into a lithe, pale woman with a shock of dark curls and a full-sleeve of tattoos covering her right arm.

Nora approached the front door of the Hell Bar, slid the keys into the lock. Langford shushed me, focused on trying to make out the things Nora said or did to bypass the wards. Hell Bar's security didn't look overly tough. Two entrances; one to the main club, another to the beer garden. More access via the loading dock on the bottom floor of the Oasis center that the bar suckled against like a lungfish on a shark. The bouncers were regulation issue; big guys, all shoulders, in dark shirts and slacks.

You could kid yourself into thinking it'd be an easy job until Nora showed up, pausing in front of the double-doors to whisper to herself and spill a pinch of salt across the threshold of her joint. Langford made notes in the ragged moleskin where things got puzzled out.

The bar opened and Nora disappeared inside. Langford logged the time, every staff member she interacted with. The ravens did the same.

"Keep an eye on 'em, eh?" I said, nodding to the birds.

"Ah-huh." Langford didn't look up from her scribble. She chewed on a pencil and frowned.

"I mean it," I said. "They could be—"

Langford glanced up, her expression set. "You want to back out on the job, trigger, say the word and I'll leave all this glamor behind."

I shook my head. "It's not about backing out."

"Course not," Langford said. "You're just the kind of unprofessional fucker who gets up your partners ass for the fun of it, then?"

I opened my mouth to argue. Shut it again, right smart. "Fine," I said. "I'm making tea. You want something?"

Langford nodded and went back to her notes, getting lost in the work. After leaving the black coffee at her elbow, I retreated to the couch and dug my copy of *Persuasion* out of my pack.

Langford stopped giving me shit about the ravens when they didn't leave. They were still perched on the wire on Saturday night, surveilling the Hell Bar like black feathered cops on a stakeout. I'd come to my senses and cleared out of the apartment, headed back to the safe house to sleep and prepare, but Langford called me a little after nine o'clock and asked me to check something out.

The Hell Bar was a different beast on a Saturday night. It attracted a younger crowd: jeans, ragged t-shirts, hairstyles that caused bosses and parents alike to lament the provocative choices of the young. Less polished than your standard club crowd on the Coast, a little wilder around the edges. The DJ's music bled across the mall, a mixture of old-school metal and punk.

Langford let me into the apartment, pushed the binoculars into my chest. "End of the mall," she said. "Below your goddamn birds. You aren't going to miss him."

I looked. Found the sorcerer right where she said he'd be, loitering in the shadows just outside the street lights, eyes closed as he smoked a cigarette and communed with the birds on a wire above him. I recognized him on sight. Mid-thirties. Bearded. Tight black t-shirt over a Gold Coast tan. The asshole from the Hard Rock, except this time he wasn't playing it subtle.

"Showed up with a team of five about an hour ago," Langford said. "He's been sending his boys into the club, one by one, slipping 'em past the bouncers. I crosschecked details with the log—they're working to infiltrate."

"Shit," I said.

"You know him?"

"He tried to take a piece out of me, back when I first arrived."

"Right. Fuck." Langford scrubbed both hands along her face, trying to rub away the exhaustion. Her mind ticked over, sorting through possible the reasons the sorcerer could be here. None were good news.

I stood, pulled the SIG from its holster. "Tell me about his crew."

Langford started as she realized what I had planned. "The fuck I will," she said.

"He's scouted the place," I said. "He's sent his boys in. Letting him kill or capture Otto isn't going to do shit for keeping me on Sabbath's good side. Tell me about the guys inside."

"Five. Younger blokes. They wear those t-shirts like it's a uniform, jackets a little too heavy for the weather," Langford said. "All of them did the salt thing, while they waited in line, so they know enough to bypass a ward."

"You figure they succeeded?"

"Bouncers let 'em in." Langford surveyed the street. "He's waiting for something."

"Right." I checked the safety on the SIG and slipped it into the holster. "Best you pull out. I think this job's off."

Langford hesitated, glancing at the window. "Yeah?"

"Yeah," I said.

"And what's your plan, going in without a sorcerer to back you up?"

"Figured I'd have a word with our friend with the beard."

"You sure that's smart?"

"Not at all. But I don't like the coincidence, eh?"

She nodded, and I returned the nod on my way out of the apartment. I used the fire-door and descended two stairs at a time. My footsteps echoed against the concrete walls, and the stairwell reeked of urine and stale nicotine. I hit the ground floor and stepped out into the lobby, kept my pace steady as I crossed the street.

The sorcerer stood beside a gray SUV, a cigarette hanging from his lips. He glared the club with a terrible focus, never blinking, and I could feel the slight tug of something happening inside as I got close. His flunkies, taking a position in dark corners, tethering themselves to the Gloom. Dangerous to do, but they were attempting to be subtle, getting themselves all set up before the boss-man followed them in.

I came around on his blind side, threading along the back of the parking lot. Made it within three car lengths before one of the ravens cawed a warning. The sorcerer turned, cigarette held between two fingers. Spotted me hovering beside a red hatchback with faded paintwork.

I eased out of the cover, SIG in hand. No point trying to hide once you've been identified.

"Last time I ran into you, my friend messed up your arm," I said. "Trust me when I tell you, I'm a better shot."

He snorted and flicked his cigarette aside. Stepped away from SUV, both hands exposed. "So, you'd be Keith Murphy," he said. "Don't worry. I know your rep, sir."

"Wish I could say the same."

"As it should be," the sorcerer said. "I prefer to work low-key."

"Humor me. Give me a name."

"Well." He smirked at me, fingers open. "Call me Thirteen."

"I've called people dumber things."

"I'm sure you have." He glanced down at the SIG. "That's a beautiful firearm. How long do you think you can wave it around before somebody freaks out and cops show up?"

"I dunno. It's nice and dark 'round here." I edged a little closer, lowered the gun. "Put your hands down, Thirteen. I don't need to look like I'm mugging you."

"I'd prefer to keep them up. A better chance someone will notice and all that jazz." He grinned at me, all confident. "Unless you'd elect to shoot me, just to get me to comply."

I kept the SIG trained on him, covered the space between us. "It's tempting," I said. "Real tempting."

Then I kicked him between the legs, let the pain do its job. Thirteen doubled over, hands dropping to clutch at his damaged privates. I grabbed a hank of his greasy hair, used it to haul him upright and jab the barrel of my pistol into the hollow of his throat.

"You've got five men inside that club. I can already feel them tethering. Do you want to tell me what they're doing, or do we skip to the part where this gets messy."

Thirteen grimaced. "You aren't this stupid, Murphy."

"People keep telling me that. I'm not sure where they got the idea," I said. "Roark's the smart one. I don't know shit about you, or which curses you've set up to chase me when after you're dead. Don't rightly care, either. What I do is plug people until they stop moving."

"Idiot," Thirteen said, and I felt something cold and sharp stick into my neck. Pain burned through my muscles, jammed them tight. One of Thirteen's flunkies stepped into my field of vision, a grin plastered over his face. He held up a silver needle, point beaded with thin tendrils of shadow that writhed around the metal. A simple paralytic spell, a rookie sorcerer's trick.

I'd gotten overconfident and paid the price for it.

"To answer your question, Mister Murphy, we were sitting on the bar in the hopes you'd show up. Local whispers say you and Nora Otto have a history, and our other attempts to track you proved ineffective." Thirteen straightened, took a tentative step, favoring his groin. "A desperate ploy but we needed to find you."

My jaw ached from the effort of trying to talk back. Thirteen grinned at me, let his flunky lever the SIG from my frozen fingers. "We need the soul of Michael Wotan," he said. "You don't understand what his death has set in motion."

His flunky handed over my gun and rifled through my pockets, searching for the soul cage or some clue of where I'd hidden it. There wasn't much to find beyond the keycard for the apartment we'd used in the stakeout, and the small bundle of cash to cover cabs and incidental expenses. The flunky gave everything over, and Thirteen's smile wilted on the vine.

"I'm not sure what he's done, but I'd advise you to step aside." A low voice, soft and feminine, speaking from a point somewhere behind my head. I recognized it straight away. Sixteen years hadn't changed it that much. "I don't doubt he earned it, whatever you've got planned, but I guarantee you, he's pissed me off worse."

Thirteen arranged his face into a pleasant grin. "Miss

Otto," he said. "We're not looking to interfere in your business."

"Five punk sorcerers come into my bar, disrupt the wards and start juicing up in the shadows like they're aiming to cause trouble. Forgive me if I don't take you at your word." Nora stepped forward, just inside my field of vision. Still wearing her leather skirt, a vintage Pistol's t-shirt with a blazer over the top, a discrete .32 nestled in her hand. "I'd consider it as a kindness if you gave Keith back his voice now."

The flunky put his body between Thirteen and Nora Otto's gun. "You don't understand," he said. "The killer must—"

Nora whipped the gun across the flunky's nose. The weapon blurred, split the skin open. The flunky dropped hard, fingers going to his face, the silver needle bouncing off the bitumen. My jaw twitched. Muscles unclenched, aching from the prolonged effort. It was all I could do to keep on my feet.

Thirteen had a phone in his hand, pulled from his pocket while Nora dealt with the flunky. He held it in a tight grip, thumb hovering over the keypad. "I don't think you comprehend the depths of shit that await you," he said. "I have need of Mister Murphy. I cannot allow you to interrupt us."

"And yet, I've got the gun," Nora said. "And I doubt you've got any hoodoo that'll save you."

I tried to warn her, but my throat wasn't up to it. The best I managed was a deranged croak. Thirteen smiled. Nora saw the phone. She fired as he mashed his thumb against the keypad.

The bar exploded outwards, dark flames filling the night with a wash of hot air. It wasn't entirely natural. It wasn't entirely magic. Part of me respected that, even as the blast wave knocked us all to the ground.

THE SECOND HIT

People screamed. Thirteen was sprawled across a car bonnet, bleeding from the stomach. Crawling to the safety of the Gloom. My SIG gone, tucked into some place in the shadows of his jacket. Nora Otto lay on the ground, eyes closed, her .32 dropped amid the chaos. My arms and legs protested as I crawled after the sorcerer.

My ears rang, unable to focus on anything but the screaming and the echo of the explosion's roar. Thirteen reached into the darkness, pulled out something tangible and dark. It wrapped around him, tendrils lashing onto his arm and drawing him in.

I dove for Thirteen as the shadows dragged him in, came up with a handful of air. Someone called my name. It sounded dim and far away, lost among the cacophony of screams and oncoming sirens.

"Murphy, come on." This time Langford's voice cut through the din, calling me to the van. She'd parked on the edge of the lot, swung the door open with practiced ease. The engine still rumbled, ready to pull off at speed, and there weren't any good reasons to stay. I grabbed Nora and got my shoulder beneath her weight, forced my aching body to haul us both towards the vehicle.

It wasn't an elegant dive into the van—more a lurching stumble that ended with Nora and I tangled together as my ribs hit steel. Langford didn't bother waiting for the door to shut, pulling out the moment she realized we were in. There were sirens nearby, too close for comfort, and Langford floored the accelerator to put distance between us.

"Thought I told you to pull out."

"I owed you," Langford said. "Didn't spot the ravens in time. I don't enjoy being wrong."

"Cheers," I said.

"You're welcome." She took a hard corner, swung us onto the highway. Eased back to the speed limit, so we attracted less attention, checking the rear-view for a tail. "What in fuck happened?"

"Someone was luring me out of hiding," I said. "He got inventive when Nora interrupted our discussion."

"Nora, as in, the target?"

"That'd be the one," I said. "We'll need a safe place to stay. Somewhere a little more secure than the safe house. They jabbed me with a Gloom pin to keep me paralyzed. Purging will take it out of me, and Nora's unconscious, probably hurt—"

"It's okay," Langford said. "I've got a spot in mind."

"Weapons," I said. "Asshole took my gun. I've set up a stash years ago, but—"

"I'm on it," Langford said.

Langford drove us out to the Valley, up close to the national park where they used to log cedar in the days before the Coast was a city. There were remnants of colonial logging camps hidden in the bush, but the bulk of the Valley was given over to small farms and forest getaways. Langford's place sat right up the back, high on the slopes of the mountains. Her veranda overlooked a good kilometer of the winding road, plus a herd of disinterested cows in the paddocks on the far side.

We got Nora into Langford's spare room, then I crashed out on her threadbare couch with one arm thrown across my face. I slept fitfully, woke a little after dawn. A gentle rain tapped the corrugated roof of Langford's home. An ancient, analog clock said it was five-eleven in the AM, and the old familiar instincts told me trouble was coming. Langford padded out from the bedroom as I put on my shoes. She carried a worn, well-cared for .303, handed me the rifle without a word. I checked the lever action, joined her at the sliding door that led out to the balcony. A black sedan parked at the edge of her property, just outside the boundary line where her wards began.

We eyed the car for a couple of minutes. Finally, I asked: "Thirteen or Sabbath?"

"Sabbath," Langford said. She picked up a dreadlock and toyed with the end. "It feels like demons."

"Your wards are that good?"

"Better."

It might have been bravado, but it was a comforting thought. "How long they been there?"

"I felt them arrive before sunrise," Langford said. "Figured the wait wouldn't hurt them any, since you were still sleeping."

"Right. I'll go take care of it." I shouldered her rifle, headed for the back door.

"They can't get in," Langford said. "Not without making the kind of noise Sabbath tries to avoid."

"What's in the gun?"

"Bullets," Langford said. "Nothing fancy about them, trigger. I don't go picking fights with the local demon tribes."

"Ah-huh."

Her eyes narrowed. "Hope you aren't thinking about messing that up for me."

"That depends."

"On what?"

"On how well-informed they are."

I let myself out and trudged down the steep driveway, struggling to keep my feet. There was two hundred meters between Langford's place and the main road, all of it downhill. A hard trek, especially in the wet, with slippery mud beneath your boots. Rainwater dripped into my eyes and the flannel shirt clung to my chest. I focused on keeping a good grip on the rifle, carried it under one arm like a hunter out for a stroll. No point in leveling it right off the bat, leaving them no choice but to go defensive.

Wesna and Randall stood beside the low-set Holden, giving themselves six feet before they'd hit the fence. Randall held an umbrella in place, every inch of him tall and prissy. Wesna just put faith in her jacket, let the rain slick her dark hair against her forehead.

"So I hear Nora's bar went boom last night," she said.

"Righto."

"Sabbath asked us to track you down, find out what you know."

"Sensible." I adjusted the grip on the .303, made sure I could get it up in a hurry.

"Don't give us shit." Randall took an angry step forward, but Wesna caught his arm and hauled him into line.

"This isn't a pleasant kind of morning," she said. "Any chance we can come in, talk things out over coffee and warm biscuits? All nice and reasonable." She smiled pleasantly, like it wasn't raining out. Like she wouldn't be putting a fist through my face if the wards on Langford's property kept her from approaching.

"I don't mind the rain," I said. "Reminds me I'm alive."

Randall produced a knife, surging forward on a wave of anger. "You fucking cu—"

I got the .303 up, leveled at his head. Wesna gripped his shoulder again, fingers cinching tight. "Don't." Her voice stayed low and controlled. "Mister Murphy here is a professional. You will treat him like one."

Randall glowered at me, lowered the knife to his side. I kept the rifle up.

"Apologize," Wesna said.

Randall mumbled something that could have been an apology, or a promise to cut out my damn tongue. The rain made it hard to tell, but either way, Wesna removed her hand. She offered me a pleasant smile. "So the first thing we should check: is Nora Otto dead?"

"That's what you hired me to do," I said.

"You honestly expect me to accept that answer?"

"Depends," I said. "You really want to start this conversation by telling me I'm unprofessional?"

Wesna stared. Randall fumed beneath his umbrella. The rain kept falling on all of us. "Okay," Wesna said. "We'll come back to that one. Let's move on to the explosion."

"Not my idea."

Randall barked out a short laugh. "No shit it wasn't your idea."

I tapped an irritated finger against the stock of the .303. "You wanted these done quiet, so the blame could be portioned off to others. I still had another week before Otto should have been dead, I was figuring a way to do it smooth and easy."

"And?"

"And a third party got involved. I ended up improvising."

"I figured," Wesna said. "You'll have to forgive Randall. Friends of his frequented the bar. They were present when what happened, happened."

"So, what, you hoped you'd threaten me a little? See if I could bring 'em back?"

"We're not here to make threats." Wesna pushed wet hair away from her face, her smile showing teeth for the first time since the conversation started. "There doesn't seem much point. You've retreated to a place of moderate safety, acquired an ally of considerable power in the form of Miss Langford. Not that breaking in there is beyond our capabilities, but we're reasonable people, Murphy." She glanced at Randall. "Most of us, at least."

She paused, hoping I'd comment. I let the rain fill the silence for me, adjusted my stance in the muddy soil. It takes effort to train a gun on someone for a prolonged conversation. The Enfield .303 weights about four kilograms. No one wants to hold that weight at their shoulder for five straight minutes.

"Here is the question that's bothering me," Wesna said. "You're not responsible for the explosion. This corroborates many of the details we've heard, looking into the incident and getting copies of the police report. Miss Otto isn't listed among the dead, which means you're either misleading us about her death or very good at your job."

"I'm not lying," I said.

"I said we'd come back to that." Wesna brushed water out of her eyes, sighed into the rain. "You performed well on that first appointment, Murphy. We gave you the target, and the target disappeared. No sign of their deaths to upset with the mortal cops. No ghosts hanging 'round in the Gloom 'causing trouble for the rest of us. I can appreciate that kind of work. I know how hard it is. Sabbath appreciates that approach, but he isn't happy. There's no confirmation of Otto's death, and an unexpected variable is creative waves. Explosions aren't how we do business."

"It wasn't my fault," I said. "A third party stepped in."

"You really want me to tell Sabbath you brought a new player into his city?" Wesna shook her head. "Thirteen's a disciple of Michael Wotan, and we know what happened in Adelaide when you and your partner fucked up. I protected you when he first showed up, shared none of my suspicions when he jumped you at the Hard Rock. Sabbath won't be pleased to learn about that. He's already willing to expend resources on Miss Langford's wards, getting a team of his less savory employees in to make a mess of things. Neither of us wants that."

"I do," Randall said. He'd retreated to the car, leaned his weight against it. The finger I had resting against the rifle trigger itched to apply pressure, to nail the prick from under ten feet. One shot wouldn't hurt him, but six of them would do some damage. That would give me a chance to take him down for good.

Instead, I lowered the .303. Stood there in the rain, looking from demon to demon.

"You can both get fucked," I told them. "Pass it on to Sabbath. Next time I see you, I'll put a bullet in your brain. Get your asses back to the Gloom and stay there."

Wesna cocked her head. "You're in a bad mood."

"'Cause Sabbath promised me no one who'd offend my sensibilities."

"Could be he stuck by that," Wesna said. "Maybe your old friend Nora wasn't so nice as you'd like to think."

"Hasn't lost his fondness for twisting words."

"Words are the foundation of an agreement." Wesna showed off rows of neat, white teeth. "Words kept you alive, Mister Murphy, the first time you left this city. They're what's keeping you breathing right now, 'cause we've got no evidence you've reneged, despite my personal theories about the way this job went down."

Wesna's smile didn't waver, but the humor drained out of her features. "If we uncover proof that confirms my suspicions, this conversation will take a very different course."

"You're not going to find shit," I said. "Nora Otto's—"

Wesna's long, handsome face transformed into something garish and horrible. She stepped forward and raised her right hand. Slowly, very deliberately, she pressed her fingertips against the wards, testing their limits. Darkness pooled around her palm, thin wisps gathering at the point of contact, circling each finger like a tiny hurricane. No way it wasn't hurting her, given the strength of Langford's defenses.

Wesna showed no signs of pain, that hideous, empty smile plastered across her face. She glared through the film of magic forming between us. "The next time you see me, Keith, I'll have your third target. You and I will pretend this conversation never happened and behave like professionals."

She retracted the hand, worked feeling back into her fingers. The unrelenting rain forced me to blink away the water as she retreated.

"Or we'll know for sure you're lying. That won't end well."

She climbed into the car, waited patiently for Randall to close his umbrella and take the driver's side.

The storm swallowed the taillights as they drove away.

PLANS AND REMINISCENCES

I spent the rest of the day seated on Langford's veranda, watching the road. The rain came down in a torrent, relentless and constant. Round sunset Langford emerged with a pot of coffee. She put a mug on the table.

"Drink," she said. The warm, bitter scent of espresso overwhelmed all other senses. Whatever Langford brewed in her kitchen was far better than any takeaway cup she'd brought into the field.

Langford settled into the other chair and propped a foot on the balcony rail. No shoes—she preferred to be barefoot at home, and wore jeans and a long-sleeved peasant blouse to cover her ink. The dreadlocks tied back and the sharp lines of her brow and cheeks were a stark reminder of the skull beneath.

I poured a cup of coffee and nursed it, drawing comfort from its warmth. The muggy heat gave way to a chill bite, now the rain was falling.

"You see anything out there?"

I shook my head. "You?"

"Nope, but they're there. I can feel them out there, watching the place. Sabbath wants his pound of flesh."

"Sabbath doesn't worry me."

Langford ran her fingers over her jeans. "He worries me."

"Sabbath, we know. Sabbath's predictable."

"That assumption's part of the reason I worry."

"They'll let me roll out of here. They won't start a fight on your doorstep."

Langford nodded. Her eyes fixed on the horizon. "You need me to dig into Thirteen," she said. "Find out where he came from, how he fits in with Wotan and your bullet."

"I want that, but I can't ask for it. I think we've used up whatever favors you owed Roark."

"That you have," Langford said, "but I'll do it, anyway."

"The way shit's going, my capacity to repay any debts will be curtailed something vicious."

"Then let's keep it simple." Langford stood up, stretched. Thin, tattooed wrists poked free of her sleeves. "You survive this, Murphy, you owe me a favor. Seems to me you're the kind of son-of-a-bitch who remembers what he owes people."

"I just lied to a demon who used to be my best friend." I finished my coffee, put the mug on the table. "The odds of me surviving are damn low."

"I'm willing to take my chances," Langford said. "Tell me what you already know about Wotan's organization."

I drew a deep breath and laid out all the details about the hit, all the ways Roark and I assumed we'd done it neat and clean. I told her about the soul, trapped and taken. Langford listened. Nodded. Took the occasional notes.

At the end, I asked her for one last favor. "I'll take Nora with me," I said. "She needs to disappear for this to work."

"She'll go for that?"

"Probably not."

"Awful big risk, then."

"I owe her, and she's my responsibility. I've got a few days to talk her into going along with the plan. But that means there's something back at the safe house that doest have my full attention."

Langford raised an eyebrow, and I told her what I wanted. Laid out all the necessary steps to keep the soul cage secure. Langford made notes, nodding. "If you're sure," she said.

"I'm sure."

She cast her eyes down the list. "Best I get started then."

She left me standing vigil on the veranda, only emerging a few hours later to tell me Nora Otto was awake.

The sunflower print on the bedroom curtains were faded with years of use. Nora sat on the edge of an overstuffed double bed, sipping a cup of tea. I settled into a wicker chair. My arms still ached and my legs burned with the effort, but as bad as I felt, Nora looked worse. She'd caught the explosion, got tossed around, but it wasn't the physical injuries that took the real toll. She'd lost her bar. Lost employees, regulars, and customers. Me perched in the corner, watching her sip her drink, wouldn't be doing her any favors given our goddamn history.

Nora spent a long time looking at the window, studying the seam of light from the veranda peeking beneath the curtains. She turned to me; her face set and steady, determined to cope. "You should have some."

"I'm not thirsty."

"It's fantastic tea," Nora said. "Whatever else your friend's good at, she's got a knack for beverages."

"I've been awake for hours. I know what I'm missing at this point."

"Ah." Nora looked towards the open door, the living room beyond. Langford had retreated to the kitchen, giving us plenty of space. "So, you're back." She said. "When did that happen?"

"Weeks ago," I said.

"How many?"

"My return wasn't planned," I said. "Things got fucked up. I needed to lie low."

She nodded, put the tea down on the bedside table. "I get that," she said. "I remember how it was, before you bailed on me and all."

"I didn't bail. I had to leave."

Nora glared at me. Blue eyes under dark curls, burning with anger. Her jaw pulled tight as fencing wire. "You bailed," she repeated. "It took me a long time to forgive you for that, Murphy. Don't fuck it up by pretending it wasn't running away."

I kept my mouth shut. Didn't bother with any more explanations. Nora was right—I ran. Blame it on being young, stupid, and unaware of other options.

"So you came back," Nora said, "and figured you'd announce your return by bringing a shitload of trouble down on my head."

"No," I said. "I came home and cut a deal with Sabbath. Agreed to do some work for him, in exchange for a hassle free stay. I didn't plan on coming near you. I'd fucked up you and me enough for one goddamn lifetime."

"Don't play the martyr," Nora said. "It doesn't really suit you."

"You either," I said.

"What's that supposed to mean? I'm the girl you left behind."

"And I got sent to kill you," I said, "by a demon I could have sworn you didn't know existed back when you and I were dating."

Nora blinked, her blue eyes cold and hard. "Oh," she said. "We dated now?"

"Didn't we?"

"No," she said. "Not really. You and I, Murphy, we fell into each other's orbit. Dating's a terrible word for that. It implies you cared about me, instead of using me as the temporary escape when your other life got too much for you."

"Well, you were a good refuge."

Her eyes narrowed. "I saved your ass last night," she said. "Why don't you at least try to get through this without fucking insulting me."

"Okay," I said. "Why'd Sabbath want you dead?"

"I owed him," Nora said. "I wasn't paying up. Not the smartest play, I'll grant you, but I've spent the entire time since you've been gone trying to stay ahead of my debts. You know what he's like when you owe him for too long. You, better than anyone, yeah? Isn't that why you left?"

"No," I said. "Roark cleared my way out."

"Roark's your friend? The guy Sabbath's got a hard-on for?"

"That's him," I said.

She nodded. "He the one who told you to leave me behind?"

It was my turn to nod.

"Your friend Roark's an asshole," she said.

"Nora—"

"No," she said. "You don't get it. I was nineteen, Keith. My boyfriend, more or less, up and disappears. He might not have been a great partner, with all the secrets and the moody silence and the sketchy-as-fuck-friends, but he was my goddamn boyfriend and I thought I was in love."

Her voice cracked. She took a deep breath, fought to regain control. "It makes it hard, not knowing what happened, when that shit goes down. Even at nineteen, I needed answers. So I tracked down Wesna, got her help. Put all the pieces together until I found my way to Sabbath. She didn't want me going there, getting up close with him. Didn't know how to stop me, either, and your name opened up his doors 'cause he still wanted ways to hurt you and I seemed all kinds of useful in that regard."

"You shouldn't have done that."

"No fucking shit." Nora turned towards the window, watched the light growing dimmer beneath the curtain. "After a few years, I figured out you weren't coming back. By then, Sabbath had me doing little jobs. That earned me a reputation, and folks puzzled out my connection to a certain asshole I used to go out with. I threw in with Sabbath 'cause that was the safest option, considering the number of enemies you left here when you bailed."

She took a deep breath, sighed. "Sixteen years. It's a long fucking time, Murphy. Let's not pretend either of us knows jack about the other, or trade on what we had. I assume you're not planning on killing me, given that I'm still breathing here?"

"It was never going to be me. I was looking for options."

"And you elected to blow up my bar because?"

"That wasn't me."

"Oh, not you, just people who wanted you dead. Assholes who'd tracked you here and figured out we had a thing." Her voice cracked a second time, accompanied by a momentary anger that washed across her features. "I built that fucking bar, Murphy. I built it out of nothing. If you're going after the asshole who blew it up, I want to be involved."

I stood up, shook my head. "Yeah. *That's* a good idea."

Nora rolled out of bed, frowning at my sarcasm. "Like I give a fuck," she said. "I think you'll find you owe me, Murphy, and I fully intend to collect."

"You're leaving town," I said. "Same way I did. Sabbath's got reason to believe you're deceased. I'd like him to keep believing that."

"If you're taking down Sabbath, I want in on that, too."

"Look—"

Nora raised a finger.

"I don't run," she said. "That's not what I do. You present me with a problem, I figure out how to solve it. If Sabbath thinks I'm dead, that gives me an advantage. I could use an edge, Keith. I can kill that motherfucker."

"Jesus, Nora."

"Jesus, Nora, nothing."

"Do you even know how to—"

There are fourteen reliable ways of killing a body possessed by a demon. She covered eleven of them in quick succession, stumbled a little over the twelfth.

"I'm not the girl you left behind," Nora said. "I figured this shit out, and I don't need saving."

"Okay," I said.

"What I need," she said. "What I've needed for a long damn time, are allies who aren't afraid to work alongside me."

She backed away from me, sat down on the bed. Reached for the kettle on her bedside table. "So… you planning to be my ally, Keith? Or you really think you can convince me I gotta slink off after all the shit you've pulled?"

THE RIGHT CALL

We left Langford's place a few hours after sunset, followed the winding route out of the Valley until we saw the lights of the suburbs. We'd been on the road about five minutes when the headlights appeared in the rearview, keeping to a safe distance. A professional would have chased me, forced me to take a corner at speed. Deaths happened all the time on the bends of narrow roads, particularly when it's wet, but that's not how demons do things. They're creatures of another era, obsessed with killing you face-to-face.

Nora sat in the passenger seat, nursing Langford's .303. She'd abandoned the leather skirt for a pair of Langford's jeans, hidden the bandages on her arm and shoulder underneath a borrowed sweatshirt. Langford used a little magic to disguise Nora's features. For the moment, she looked older, dreadlocked and pierced. From a distance, you'd mistake her for Langford. Up close, the glamor would be obvious to anyone tethered to the Gloom.

Nora didn't care. Her eyes stayed on the road, fingers tight against the gun. She said nothing until we hit the main roads and I turned onto the highway.

"North?"

"Yeah."

"That's heading towards Sabbath's territory," she said. "And we've already got a tail."

"Necessary evil," I said. "Unless you're confident we can do this with a borrowed rifle, and a rented van."

Nora buttoned her lip, but her judgment permeated the silence. I did my best to set it aside and remember the route to my stash.

The storage unit was a hold-over from my demon days, established when the idea of leaving Sabbath's employ first took seed. Housing estates surrounded the once-isolated complex, courtesy of the advancing urban sprawl. Thirty minutes to up the highway, another ten navigating the winding maze of the rental facility. I'd paid for a space deep in a multi-story structure, a two-meters-by-three deal secured by a deadbolt and enough pre-paid rent to keep five years in advance.

No signs of interference. Everything stacked as I left it: lots of boxes; old furniture, decades out of date. Dust and damp and a single, overworked light bulb that gave us a bare minimum of illumination. I pointed Nora towards a box by the door. "Grab the flashlight on the top layer," I said. "It'll have about three grand rolled up inside it, where the batteries would go."

She knelt and searched, sneezing as the dust rose. "An actual torch be more useful at this point."

"True," I said, "but we've got what we've got."

I raided the hiding places and unearthing the tools of the trade. Vials of holy water. A couple of sharp knives, one blessed by a priest and another by a local wiccan. A twelve gauge and three boxes of shells. Two P220s, earlier models of the SIG that I'd used to kill Wotan, along with ammunition for each. I loaded the first, slid it into my empty holster. Offered the second to Nora.

"Shit," she said, "weren't you the boy scout."

I looked around the cluttered shed, compared my early plans to the skills I'd picked up from Danny Roark. "This? This is nothing. Pick any other city where I keep a stash, and I can go to war with the gear I've got there."

We climbed back into the van, drove down to the McDonald's at the end of the block. Wesna and Randall parked their car outside, doing their best to look inconspicuous. Nora peeled a twenty off the roll of bills from the storage shed and ordered us some food. Quarter pounders. French fries. Cardboard cups full of Coke. I kept my eyes on the demons. Nora focused on her burger. She chewed slowly, took regular sips, mimicking Langford's birdlike movements. "So, the asshole who blew up my bar?"

"He goes by Thirteen."

"If you say so. I'll stick with asshole."

"Sure."

"What's he after?"

"Me," I said.

"That's the short version. I want something longer."

"Not certain what else there is. He's part of a cult. I killed their leader. They've been chasing me ever since."

"That's why you came back?"

"Ah-huh." I sipped my drink. The post-mix hadn't blended with the soda water, left the Coke tasting bland. Nora sat there, chewing. When she swallowed, she put the burger down. Watched me for a moment, then said: "Who else did you kill?"

I shrugged.

"Does that mean you don't know, or you don't want to tell me."

"It means it's what I do. What I've been doing for years now," I said. "Me and Roark eliminated folks who messed with things they shouldn't. Entities from the Gloom who refused to play by mortal rules. I don't feel the need to apologize for it."

"Was that your job while you lived here?"

"No," I said. "It happened afterward."

"Is it why you left?"

"One reason."

"What are the others?"

I drew a long breath. "Youth. Stupidity. My own little fuck-up while handling Sabbath's business, which meant the other option was sticking around and getting dead. Roark came along and offered an alternative. I took it because it was easy."

"Are you sorry?"

"Do we have to do this?"

"Are you sorry you bailed?"

The rain was easing up outside and moonlight peeked through the clouds. "No," I said. "I'm not sorry I left. It was the right call, Nora. I know I'm not meant to say that, but it's the honest-to-god truth."

I dragged my eyes away from the window, met her angry stare. Nora reached for her Coke, pulled it closer. Her gaze flicked to the counter, studying the strangers lined up to order. Then Nora looked at me, her eyes big and very blue. She'd given up crying a long time ago. I could see that in her face. That didn't mean she'd stopped wanting too. It didn't mean she wouldn't be crying now, if she still had tears left.

I couldn't blame her. I had plenty of regrets myself.

"Come on," I said. "We gotta find some place to crash tonight."

. . .

Traffic on the Gold Coast is a pain in the ass. It's a long, narrow city with the kind of public transport system that hugs the beach. If you want to go most places, you're driving the two arterial streets. In an urban district of six hundred thousand people, that shouldn't be a big deal. Factor in the ten million who pass through every year, it quickly adds up to a nightmare.

We lost sight of Wesna's sedan about an hour after we left McDonald's, but I took backstreets for another forty-five minutes to be sure. Dumped the van down in the Tweed, caught one of the local busses north, and checked into a hotel. We looked like hell, but the bloke behind the counter didn't bat an eye. He passed me the swipe cards and delivered a pre-packaged monolog about the complimentary breakfast buffet.

Nora sulked as we rode the elevator to the fourteenth floor. Our balcony offered a wide view of the beachfront and the dark mass of ocean. The windows were tinted, double-glazed glass, designed to help combat the heat. Nora eyed the bed in the center of the room. It was big and wide and entirely overstuffed with blankets. She sat on it and hit the remote for the TV. A cheerful, smiling woman worked out on some revolutionary exercise machine that hooked over a door. Nora watched it while I stowed my gear.

"So, where are you planning to bunk?" she said.

"The bed seems appropriate."

"And I sleep where?"

"We can switch out, nap in turns. I don't sleep much anymore, especially not with someone hunting me. I'll trust you not to run."

"Jesus, Murphy." She curled her legs up, hugged them to her body. I went to work securing the room. Basic wards on the doors and windows, powered by a few drops of blood. Then I fished a book out of my pack, settled in to the room's single armchair. I kept the SIG P220 close, resting on my lap, and opened to an unread page of *Persuasion*. I read the same passage about Anne Elliot's time at Uppercross a half-dozen times, not really able to concentrate on it. My brain ran on a loop, working through everything that'd happened. Wesna. Nora. Sabbath. Michael Wotan down in Adelaide and his friend Thirteen. I didn't like not having a plan. I hated not having Roark around to think details through for me.

"Murphy?" The way Nora said my name, all soft and gentle, did more to get my attention than the word itself. She'd crawled into bed wearing a t-shirt Langford had loaned her, left her jeans in a small puddle with her belt and her shoes beside them. Her head was resting against the pillow, stray hairs falling across her face. The glamor faded. She looked like Nora again.

"This thing you did," she said. "This business with Roark. Tell me about it."

"There's nothing to know," I said. "Not really."

"It's—" she hesitated, bit her lower lip. "This is the job you chose over me," she said. "Give me something, yeah?"

I thought about that. Figured it couldn't hurt. Started telling her about the last sixteen years. Nora lay in the bed, watching me. I stared out the window, mouth working on its own, meandering through the training and the hits and the little details that wore away at me. The targets we'd taken down to forge a secure world: an incubus running brothels down in Kings Cross; a handful of werewolves up north, hunting the local backpackers who wandered into the bush. I dredged up the isolation of living in hotels and safe houses. The hours of setting things up. The painstaking rituals required to keep something dead, despite the Gloom-born's habit of returning from the grave.

I told Nora about Michael Wotan in Adelaide. The way Roark told me we were hitting the necromancer, the chill that shot through me at the thought of undertaking it. The hope it would finally be the end.

I told her about the cult he built up over centuries, the girls that disappeared every lunar cycle. About the pall that hung over Adelaide, Australia's own capital of murder and serial killers, all because he lived there and clung on like a tick. I mentioned Roark's instructions, the clear moon overhead that night before I broke in and pulled the trigger. About the little things I couldn't quite remember that may have been mistakes, about having to run with the soul in the bullet despite the fact I didn't really know what to do with it.

I told her all of it, 'cause she'd asked me to, and 'cause some part of me thought I owed her and hoped it might change things. Nora gave me the space to talk, the blankets pulled to her shoulders and her expression serious.

When the words petered out, I sat there and studied her face in the lamplight. The old feelings nagged at me, and I wondered what me and Nora could have become if I'd stayed. In the warm glow of what-might-have-been, all my visions of our lives played out happily, ignoring the threats and dangers being with me entailed.

"Murphy?" Nora said.

I shook off my reverie. "Yeah?"

"We're adults," Nora said. "You can use the damn bed."

"I'm okay," I said. "I won't sleep for a while."

"Murphy," she said, like I was missing something, and then I caught her eye and I put my book down and shucked off my pants while she watched. I peeled off my shirt and Nora's eyes followed the scars and the tattoos, trying to read the lost years between the lines they'd left on my body. I didn't give her long to do that, not before I was under the covers alongside her, throwing an arm around her and pulling her close. Nora wriggled back, ground her butt against my groin. I didn't protest, and she didn't complain when parts of me started remembering the times we were more than friends.

She rolled over and pressed her lips against mine. Her

hand went lower, searching for a way into my underwear. I pulled away. "Are you sure?"

Nora's fingers found what they were looking for, and after that my focus wasn't on questions or talking. We peeled off our clothes and remembered what it was like when things weren't so complicated and she didn't really hate me, and I remembered what it was like to care about something other than the job.

The next morning, I rented a sky blue hatchback and drove us both down to the safe house. The rain had cleared overnight, replaced by the clear light of morning, and the view from the house stretched out across the water. Nora spent a few minutes exploring the place, whistled beneath her breath. "Doing what you do pays better than I expected," she said. "Maybe you were right to bail."

I shook my head, promised her my usual spots for lying low involved more fleas and less impressive views. "This is Langford's doing," I said. "She knows people with money who owe her favors."

"Good for her." Nora strolled over to the window, rested her forehead against it. She was still wearing the borrowed jeans, coupled them with a sweater we'd picked up at the gift-shop below the hotel. "You think her friends have got something a little less conspicuous hanging around in their wardrobe?"

"Good odds," I said. "Bedroom's through and to the left."

Nora nodded and disappeared into the bedroom, leaving me alone in the kitchen. I took a few moments to check the wards, then made coffee. We hadn't mentioned the events of the previous evening. I wasn't sure if I should have started that. I drained my coffee as Nora emerged, wearing a too-large t-shirt that hung over her jeans.

"Langford has big friends," she said.

"Sorry," I said.

"You sure this Thirteen asshole will have my apartment covered?"

"If they don't," I said. "Sabbath will. Either of them is liable to take a shot at you, given the circumstances."

"I'll need clothes, Murphy."

"We'll get to that," I said. "This'll get us by, 'til we can sort a better option. Priority is making sure they buy your death, while we keep us from getting dead. That matters more than the size of your shirt."

I handed her a coffee. Black. Two sugars. The way she'd drunk it as a teenager. Nora sipped it, winced at the flavor, but she said nothing. I watched her pace around the lounge room, then settle into the couch.

"So here's the deal," I said. "You wait here for a day. Lie low. Watch some TV. Raid the refrigerator when you get hungry and all. Just stay out of sight and don't breech the wards. They've kept me safe this long, with Thirteen looking for me, and Sabbath hasn't seen fit to come down here and blow the place up, which is a good sign they don't know I've been staying here."

"And you?"

"I'll talk to an old friend," I said. "See if I can undo some of the mess I've made of your goddamn life in the last twenty-four hours, then see if I can get a lead on Thirteen so I can dissuade him from further acts of terrorism against people I used to know."

"You think you can do that?"

I pulled a knife we'd recovered from the storage shed, tapped my fingers against the older SIG P220 in my holster. "I plan on being convincing," I said. "It brings people around."

I left her sitting at the kitchen table, nursing a cup of coffee. Nora smiled as I left, like she was already thinking of me coming home. For a moment, I let myself believe it.

TRUST

I dialed Wesna's number and asked her to meet me. Just her, no Sabbath, no Randall riding shotgun. She called me an idiot, informed me a private chat wasn't possible, then suggested I go get lost.

I took the rental car down to the Palm Beach/Currumbin bridge, parked alongside an old RSL club. The walking paths following the creek. I followed them over to the far shore, headed towards the see until the path veered through the remnants of the mangroves, concrete giving way to wooden decks that cut between thin clumps of trees. I followed the curve, found a seat in this covered alcove tucked away about half-way along the decking. A lookout, invisible from the nearest shore, with a picnic table looking downriver.

The brackish water sloshing against tree roots reeked of gasoline, inheriting the smell from the river. As teens, Wesna and I got drunk here, and kids today continued the tradition. The small trash can overflowed with empty bottles and beer cans. I could make out the wide expanse of Currumbin Bridge through a space in the trees. Behind it, the slope of Currumbin Hill that watched over the suburbs instead of the goddamn beach.

The waiting got to me pretty quick. I stuck my hands in my pockets and wondered what Nora was doing right now. Ran through her story about owing Sabbath money, testing its details for truth. I'd started theorizing about other possibilities when Wesna showed up, coming around the bend at a light jog. She'd dressed down for the occasion. Sneakers. Sweat pants. A plastic visor protecting her face. Just another Gold Coast fitness freak running the mangrove path.

She came to a stop, hands on her hips. Her expression wasn't friendly. "For real," she said. "Is Nora Otto dead?"

I stared at her, saying nothing.

"I should wring your neck," she said. "Twist your skull free of that annoying carcass and take it back to Sabbath as a trophy."

"You should." I grinned at her, wry and careful. Hoped she'd recognize it as a joke, instead of tacit permission. "I mean, this? This isn't smart, Wes'. Not wise at all, goddamnit."

"Don't blaspheme." Her expression didn't budge. "And this is against-my-better-judgment shit, Murphy. Try not to push it, okay?"

"Deal." We stood, facing each other, listening to the mosquitoes and the river and the distant sound of traffic. I backed off before her, retreating to the wooden seat. Wesna watched, arms folded, waiting.

"I wouldn't have picked you for a jogger," I said.

Her expression grew severe.

"Right, business." I drew a long breath, exhaled. "First up, I need to figure out, you know, given what's gone down here—"

"No," Wesna said.

"No?"

"Not at any price you're willing to give him," she said. "You fucked a job. That's it. He'll set the hounds on you, revel in your damn pain. That was always the plan, though. I assume you predicted that."

"I did."

Wesna took off the visor, studied me as I watched the river. "Why ask, then?"

"I enjoy knowing where I stand. It makes it easier to figure out which moves are really there," I said. "Shit'll get rough, sooner than you think, and having Sabbath on my team doesn't seem like a bad idea."

"You dream big," Wesna said.

"That I do." I crouched, picked up a discarded bottle cap from the debris on the platform. I lined it up on my index finger, sent it spinning into the creek with my thumb. "So what's he offering Nora, that she's so willing to forgive me?"

Wesna raised an eyebrow, half-amused at the prospect. "Maybe it's your natural charm?"

"We both know I'm not that charming."

"True, but Sabbath can't offer Nora Otto anything that makes forgiving and forgetting a worthwhile proposition."

"I'm betting he can," I said, "especially given the situation. She came to him after I left, offered to work for him in exchange for knowledge. He knew the connection to me. Kept her in the back pocket, playing a long game in case the opportunity for revenge presented itself. You're not going to tell me such a thing's beyond his capabilities?"

"It's not," Wesna said.

"So?"

"That's not his play here," she said. "He set her as a target to hurt you, sure, but that wasn't the only reason. The Nora you dated, she's gone, mate. Spent too much time running the place where black market deals got done. Sabbath wanted her eliminated because she'd become a threat. Nora Otto knows secrets these days. Used them to pay off her debt years ago."

"Not the story she tells."

"No reason she should." Wesna crossed the platform,

settled her ass on the bench beside me. "The Boss isn't pissed Hell Bar went up in flames, even with the time he's putting in keeping the cops from losing their shit. Nora's joint going boom is good fucking news for him; one more up-and-comer without a power base to challenge him. And she's still a threat now, with the club gone. Nora knows too many people, accumulated favors over money. You got history with her and all, but..."

Wesna didn't finish that thought. Sabbath had sworn he wouldn't send me after anyone who didn't have it coming, and odds were good he'd lived up to that. Demons thrived on falsehood. They lied through their teeth, sweated lies out of their borrowed pores. But there weren't many that swore an oath intending to betray it.

I stood and dusted off my jeans. "If you planned on turning on me, now's the time."

Wesna shook her head. "We're a pair of old friends catching up on things. I ain't swearing to tell the truth, but I believe you're more useful alive."

"Appreciate it," I said.

"You shouldn't," Wesna said. "It makes the part where I have to hurt you sting a little worse. I'll hold that against you, when Sabbath gives the orders."

"Maybe we'll get lucky, and you won't be asked to do the hurting," I said.

"No one's got that kind of good fortune." Wesna put her visor back on her head, preparing to jog into the shadows. "I swear to God, Murphy. Not even you."

My father once rented an apartment on Burleigh Beach. We lived there three years, longer than I spent anywhere else in my childhood. It never felt like home, but it came closer to it than most. Roark claimed that's what made me good at the job. Not the sight I'd learned to ignore, or the skills I'd picked up breaking legs for Sabbath. Just my habitual refusal to belong somewhere. The roots we put down in the real world are mirrored in the Gloom, getting twisted into weapons that could get used against us.

I drove out to Burleigh and parked on the beach. Found a payphone, one of the few that still existed, and dialed the in-case-of-major-fuck-up number. It rang out twice, spitting out my change, but I fed it back in and called again.

I got an answer on the third attempt. Danny Roark said, "Keith?"

"Yeah."

"You weren't supposed to call," he said.

"Yeah."

"Then I'm assuming it's bad, and we need to make this fast," Danny said.

I studied the phone booth, the graffiti and tags scratched into the glass walls. The line snapped and popped, distorting as old copper landlines tried to connect with cell. I noticed my own breathing, in and out, marking off the empty seconds.

"Roark?"

He took a long breath. "Yeah?"

"Things are bad here," I said. "The cult tracked me here. They've got people in the city. Sabbath..."

I heard the click of a cigarette lighter, louder and clearer than the line distortion. The pause as Roark inhaled, thinking details over.

"We both predicted Sabbath would be difficult," he said. "Wotan's minions following you was always a possibility. Stick to the plan, kid. You know what's at stake."

"No," I said. "Not really. The way Langford talks about Wotan? The way his followers are coming after me? They're blowing shit up, Danny. Attacking me in the midst of a crowd, screw the collateral damage. They don't care if they get noticed, and that ain't normal."

I left that out there, waiting for Roark to pick it up.

He didn't. Just smoked his cigarette. "Did you keep the soul cage secure?"

"Yeah, but—"

"But nothing," Roark said. "It's all that matters, Keith."

"No," I said, "it's not."

I leaned against the car, stared at the old apartment building. Listened to the waves rolling into the beach behind me. "What the fuck did we start, Danny? Just once, give me details. Treat me like a partner."

The silence that answered seemed like it would last forever. "Roark?"

"Still here."

"Come on, man. I need to know."

"Yeah."

Roark sighed, low and quiet.

"Ragnarök," he said. "Wotan's death curse was supposed to kick off an apocalypse."

I chewed on that. Absorbed it. "That's a new one," I said. "How close did he come?"

"Close enough."

Roark hung up the phone, left me alone with the beach and the dial tone.

ESCHATOLOGICAL CONSTANTS

Peer into the Gloom on the regular, and you become a student of eschatology. Ragnarök. The End of Days. The long count on the Mayan Calendar and the last days of the Kali Yuga. Myths and religions are replete with scenarios that mark the destruction of the world, and once you realize that demons and magic are real, it's not long before you do the math.

The apocalypse is inevitable. Every species of Other that emerges from the Gloom, every faction that finds its way here, believes that the end is imminent. They just disagree on how it will happen, when it arrives, and who gets to kick it off.

Very few eschatology scenarios work out well for humanity. Which makes it easy to sway people to your side once they've brushed against the Gloom and realized that something's coming.

The promise of self-preservation against inevitable catastrophe appeals to pretty much everyone.

I returned to the Currumbin Hill safe house. No sign of Nora Otto. The cold, sterile emptiness of the place suggested she'd left a while back. I fumbled for the lights, turned on the row that led down the short flight of stairs from the front door to the lounge room. I didn't bother calling Nora's name. Instinct said she'd already bailed, and all that really remained was finding out was how she'd fucked me on the way out.

They'd tossed the safe house with speed in mind. All the drawers in the kitchen opened, their contents strewn over the floor. Couch cushions torn and spread across the hardwood, ensuring there was nothing hidden within. Solid work, methodical. I checked the duffle bag we'd taken from the storage shed, discovered the knives, spare SIG P220, and cash were gone.

I drew my gun, edged my way into the bedroom. Of all the shit in the safe house, only one thing really mattered, and I knelt to retrieve the warded box from beneath the bed.

A big man emerge from the shadows. Not Thirteen, but he looked like the sorcerer's Neanderthal older brother. Huge. Bearded. Tattoos exposed for all to see, skin tanned to the consistency of leather. He grinned when I pointed the SIG at him.

"Stay," I said.

The Neanderthal hesitated, and that's all I needed from him. I put a bullet into his shoulder. The type of flesh wound that hurt like hell, reminding him of the stupidity of attempting violence against an armed opponent. Pity for me this guy ignored the memo.

There's an optimal range for firearms, and we were well inside it. The Neanderthal stepped forward, closed a meaty fist around my gun and wrenched it out of my grip.

"Hear you killed the Master," the Neanderthal said. "You trapped his soul in steel and lead."

Knuckles the size of a brick connected with the side of my face, got me seeing stars.

"You shouldn't have done that," the Neanderthal said. "The Master kept us safe."

I was down, sprawled against the bed. The Neanderthal advanced, those big ham-hock fists ready to bludgeon me into pulp. No way I could take another hit. The adrenaline kicked in, gave me enough clarity to roll free. I came up with sheets in hand, flung them at his face. The Neanderthal brought his arm up, guarding his features. Offered me an opening to hook the ribs, and I put all my weight behind it. Felt like I was punching a side of beef, not really doing shit, but I heard the Neanderthal wheeze for a moment, his breath knocked out of him.

I pulled the knife. Four inches of tempered steel, a red rubber grip. Not the kind of weapon you go out using if you're looking for a fight, but it fit in my pocket and didn't attract too many questions. The blade bit into the Neanderthal's shoulder. My second stab gashed his arm.

The Neanderthal bellowed and staggered back, blood slicking over his ink. He ground his teeth and snorted, psyching himself up to retaliate. The weapon changed the equation for him—nobody got through a knife fight without getting cut, regardless of their size and training. Any attempt to beat me to death would mean losing more bodily fluid.

It wouldn't slow him down much. A man that big has plenty of blood to lose, and lots of muscle protecting his vital organs.

The Neanderthal howled and surged forward. I changed tack, came in low and stabbed up past the waist. Caught the Neanderthal in the stomach, sliced along instead of pulling free.

That seemed to get his attention. His fist clipped my ear, knocked me loose. I went, hit the floor. The knife stayed lodged in his torso. No way to get it back without getting into his range, so I crawled for the P220 lying on the bare boards.

The Neanderthal reefed the blade free of his side. Scowled at the weapon trying to understand why I'd bother with such a thing.

By then I'd got hands on the SIG. The gun kicked three times: two rounds to the chest, one in the head. Just like Roark taught me.

The Neanderthal teetered, a falling redwood defying the rules of gravity until the very last moment. I lay there, panting, and reached for the box beneath the bed. The floorboards were already pulled up, exposing my hiding place.

No sign of the soul cage. I unearthed my phone, dialed Langford's number. "The safe house is compromised," I said. "You do what I asked?"

"Smooth as silk."

"Good," I said. "We need to talk."

I hung up. Took a last look at the carnage they'd wrecked upon the place, with or without Nora's help. Then I grabbed my gear and got the hell out. No sense waiting for the Neanderthal's back-up, or for his ghost to emerge.

Langford met me in the food court of the Southport Mall, hunkered at a raised table that looked across the river to the theme parks on the spit. She took one look at my face and put together what happened. "Gone?"

"Gone."

"Shit," she said. "I'm sorry."

"My choice to trust her, see how she'd play it," I said. "My mess to clean up, now that we know which side she's on. You bring the gun?"

Langford nodded. She pushed a small bag across the lunch table, looked away as I stowed it in my backpack. "Glad you sent me in, then," she said. "It'd suck if you owed me for having this thing for no good reason."

I nodded, felt the familiar weight of the bullet and the soul within settle around me. I'd placed my trust in Langford, asking her to create a convincing fake of the soul cage.

Something Nora could mistake for the real one in the event of betrayal. That Langford smuggled Wotan's soul out, without being tempted to use it, justified my choice.

"Tell me about Thirteen," I said. "What d'you find out?"

"A lot, and none of it happy news. My contacts assumed he was just some random sorcerer who showed up on the strip a few years back. Way I figured it, that makes him one of Wotan's first apprentices. Someone outside the chain of command of whatever cult you disrupted down there with Roark."

"What's he been doing?"

"Nothing major." Langford speared a French fry with her fork, chewed it while she thought through her notes. "Little things. Favors. The guy knows how to be discreet. Plenty of people have worked with him, or done some business. Nobody questioned where he came from, or who he served, because he avoided going big. Thirteen focused on consolidation, firming up his place on the totem pole without raising the wrong kind of attention. The only surprise..."

"He didn't work with Sabbath?"

"Got it in one," she said. "Any dealings he's had with Sabbath's crew have been through intermediaries. Side-stepping all confrontations with the big dog."

"He worked through Nora?"

"A few times."

I nodded. Swore. "He's the bolt hole," I said. "Wotan sent him here to establish a foothold outside his cult, someone capable of lying low in case hunters like Roark and me came poking about."

"Which means he didn't follow you here 'cause he's been here all along," Langford said. "Hiding out here, same as you, only he's done it for a fuck-load longer."

"Any of your friends know where Thirteen lives?"

Langford speared another French fry, offered me a smile.

"He's got a mansion up on Tamborine Mountain, overlooking the city," she said.

"Expensive place to nest."

"Thirteen enjoys some extravagant tastes," she said. "Unlike you, he seems to prefer blending in with the pricey end of town, rather than staying in squalor."

"If he's been here this long, he'll be dug in," I said. "It'll take us too long to unravel his defenses, especially if Nora's on site."

Langford nodded. "You'd need an army to dig him out. The whole fucking place is teeming with cultists. I think the survivors relocated once word got out you were here."

"Well then," I said, "I guess we go get an army."

"There's only one worth getting around these parts."

"Yeah, I know. That's the bitch of it." I dabbed my mouth with the serviette, left it crumpled on the brown plastic tray. "I don't think Sabbath plays by the enemy of my enemy rule."

"Sabbaths got nothing but enemies," Langford said. "It makes life easy for him."

THE NEW DEAL

I walked into the Casino with my head held high. The security team flagged me from the moment I crossed the threshold, reported my presence up the line to Sabbath. The demons responded with the efficiency of a well-oiled machine: Wesna and Randall appeared at either end of the bar, cutting off any means of escape. Wesna schooled her features, professionally neutral about the job. Randall grinned like a kid on Christmas, taking lead as they picked me up. The big demon wanted to know why I'd come back. Met the suggestion I was giving myself up with a snort of derision.

"I've got a plan to recompense him for the fuck-up with Nora," I told him.

Randall gave me a disappointed sigh. "I thought you were professional, Murphy. This here? This is bush league." He signaled Wesna, and they both stood up. Waited for me to join them. "Come on," Randall said. "Let's talk to the big man."

They escorted me to the elevator, one demon at each shoulder. A trio of tourists fell in alongside us, but a snarl from Wesna convinced them to wait for the next car. Randall stepped in first, pressed the number for Sabbath's suite.

Wesna followed me in, planted a fist in my stomach as the doors slid shut. I doubled over, and Randall hauled me upright, exposed my ribs so Wesna could go to town.

By the time the door chimed on the twentieth, they needed to carry me out. My feet dragged as they carried me in, and the purple bruises on my chest made it hard to breathe.

Sabbath rose from the couch as we entered, scotch of glass in hand. Wesna and Randall dumped me at his sandals.

"You're a stubborn son-of-a-bitch," Sabbath said, showing off his teeth, and the smile set off something primal inside me, the same way my instincts knew to fear grinning sharks and serpents with exposed fangs. "I made you a deal in the spirit of generosity, Keith, and you come back to me after spitting in my face a second time? I promised you a world of pain. I promised you'd see what your own innards."

"Learned my lesson about Otto," I said. "Won't make—"

"No," Sabbath said. "I'm not interested in what you've got to tell me."

Then he settled into one of the big leather lounge chairs and held his drink in place. Sat there with the sun sinking into the mountains behind him, sipping from his bourbon while Randall and Wesna did the work. They took turns. Randall kicked off the proceedings with a straight right to the face, the impact tight and hard against the point where the jaw and my skull come together. Wesna bludgeoned the soft part of my belly, kept working it until I spat blood on Sabbath's tiled floor. I attempted to make a show of it. Tried to stay on my feet and meet Sabbath's glare, to prove he couldn't break me.

Sabbath cracked a grudging smile at my bravado, but we both knew there wasn't much backing it up. "You two, go to town," he said.

Wesna and Randall threw me to the ground and kicked

ten kinds of shit out of me. Sabbath nestled into the couch to watch, enjoying each bloody cut and groan.

I lost track of time pretty damn fast. Maybe I blacked out a little. Maybe I didn't. It'd been light outside when they started, and now the windows behind Sabbath were dark. I know because Randall was down on one knee, jerking my head up by the ears so I could meet Sabbath's stare.

"You're not allowed to die yet, Murphy."

I held a strange hope he was wrong. They'd beaten me hard, but all my internal organs were still inside me. They just wanted to be sure I'd be conscious when they started cutting.

Sabbath's cold eyes studied me, calculating his next step.

My next move was easy. I passed the fuck out.

I came to as someone attempted to force water down my throat. My lips wouldn't cooperate, too swollen and bloody. My attempt to cough the mouthful up triggered more activity from the other. Strong hands hauling me upright. A deep voice giving orders. "Come on, asshole. Drink."

I opened my mouth to object, but all I managed was a moan. And moaning hurt. Worse, it gave the asshole with the glass an opening to force more water on me. I swallowed. Gagged. Wished I could go back to the dark, sleepy place where I'd been for god knows how fucking long.

I processed my situation, on instinct. It didn't take long. Pain, followed by more pain, and then the queasy blur as my nervous system was overwhelmed. Prying my eyelids open stung. Closing them hurt too, but at least I didn't want to hurl.

The glass was at my lips again, and this time the pangs of thirst broke through the haze of suffering. I forced my bloodied mouth to swallow before they drowned me. The first mouthful went down painfully, the taste of iron on my tongue. The flavor lingered after the water pulled away. Blood, I figured. A missing tooth.

They'd dropped me somewhere warm and humid. My skin coated in a slick, stickier layer after several hours of perspiration.

"—need to rehydrate," the voice was saying, glass back at my lips. "He ain't decided to kill you yet, and that's a tiny fucking miracle. Don't give him the pleasure of dying on him now. Drink the damn water, Murphy."

I risked opening my eyes for a minute. Wesna's face emerged from the spinning blur. She'd taken off her jacket, rolled up the sleeves of her shirt.

"Try to stay awake," she said. "You may have picked up a concussion."

I tried to nod, but pain shot through my jaw. I mumbled a soft, "Hurts," into the air.

"'Course it hurts," Wesna said. "We had orders to hurt you. Randall, he took it personally. Man really doesn't like you. Think he might have broken your nose."

Soon as she mentioned it, I wanted to try sniffing and see how big a mess they'd done to my nasal passages. I forced myself to ignore that instinct, to take steady breaths through the wreckage of my mouth. Your instincts mean shit when you're beaten to all hell. After a certain point, your body just forgets how to avoid suffering. It assumes the pain is everywhere, so it falls back on the familiar instead of the smart.

"Sabbath," I mumbled.

"Sabbath ain't done with you."

"Deal—"

"The prospect of a deal's off the table," Wesna said. "You're out of things that Sabbath really wants, Murphy. Not sure you can offer anything he's interested in."

I smiled a little, even though it hurt. Whispered, "Soul," before I lowered myself back to the warm tile floor. I closed my eyes again, focused on my breathing. Wesna put her glass down. Leaned so close her breath warmed my cheek. "You offering us a soul? You really dumb enough to do that?"

"Yes." I didn't need to watch her reaction. Wesna stood and brushed her hands. I heard her boot heels clip the tiled floor as she exited.

I hurt worse than anything I'd experienced before.

Somewhere along the line, I passed out and let the darkness wash over me.

I woke up in Sabbath's lounge room. They'd washed the sticky blood away so I wouldn't stain the leather couch, patched up the worst of my injuries to keep me from passing on. Daylight streamed through the window. Sunrise. I'd been out of it for twenty-four hours or more. My body had become a fragile cardboard figure, stiff and unbending and easy to break. A demon loomed by the couch, watching me like a hawk. The moment he registered that I was awake, he disappeared through the doorway. A few moments later, Sabbath appeared. He wore a white suit with a bright carnation in the pocket. Wesna stood at his shoulder, hidden behind dark sunglasses.

I tried to lift myself off the cushions. "How long?"

"About three days." Sabbath crouched, angled forward like an eagle preparing to dive "I'm impressed with your resilience. Most people don't bounce back after Wesna and Randall beat them."

I nodded slowly. It fit. My stomach bulged with the empty, hollowed-out sensation that came from too long without a meal. "Hungry," I said.

"I'm sure you are." Sabbath folded his hands on top of his ample belly. "Question is, Murphy, do I waste food on you? No milage in feeding a mutt if you're planning to take it to slaughter in the morning."

I nodded a little to acknowledge his point. "Most people feed the dog 'cause it's humane."

"Like I've ever given a shit about humanity." Sabbath's thick tongue wormed its way across his lips. "So Wesna says you're willing to sell your soul. Tell me, Keith, is that true?"

"If the deal's good enough, I'm open to it."

"If the deal..." Sabbath grinned, delighted. "And where are you going to receive a better trade for your pitiful, blackened spirit than you'd get through me?"

"Sarcasm doesn't suit you."

"Then don't toy with me, Murphy. I kept you alive because Wesna thinks you're sincere, and I'm a businessman before anything else. That sack of meat you walk around in... all those instincts, all that physical memory. It's an appealing package, even before we take into account the little pleasures that come from having your soul to torture on a rainy day. What do you want?"

"Not here," I said.

"Here," Sabbath said. "You're not in a position to argue. Make your pitch."

I hung my head, tried to affect an air of vulnerability. It wasn't hard. They'd beaten me bad enough that I couldn't do much to fight back, and I'd never been the kind of bloke who waded into a punch-up.

"Nora Otto's been working with a cultist named Thirteen," I said. "A sorcerer, a new player in town, trained by the guy I shot down in Adelaide. They're trying to bring Michael Wotan back. I'd like your help to ensure Wotan stays dead, and whatever curse he's set upon the world is contained."

"And in exchange?"

"You get what you wanted," I told him. "Otto's eliminated. It neutralizes another potential threat before they establish a foothold. When I die, however that happens, my

soul is yours to play with and my body's a vessel your
demons can fill."

He rose, standing over me. "I like you desperate, Murphy.
It makes you... amusing."

"Do we have a deal?"

"Not yet." Sabbath's long stride ate the distance between
the couch and the door. "On the plus side, you may have
earned yourself food."

The worst part of negotiating from a position of weakness is
the waiting. When your opponent has all the leverage, they're
not in any hurry to give you an answer. They'll stretch the
hours out and let you time dwell on your position. Try to
make you realize exactly how little power you have in the
situation, hoping you'll rationalize down your expectations.
In any negotiation, whether it's for a used car or the state of
your soul, it's the person who's willing to walk away who has
the real advantage.

Sabbath's crew left me in a bare, stifling office near the
back of his suite. It should have been a nice place; the walls
were painted a light shade of sand, the floorboards were dark
and polished to a sheen. Instead, they gave the room a terrible
symmetry that didn't quite belong, and the only things that
broke it were the red leather couch and my shuffling, aching
body.

I did three slow laps, getting to know the lay of the land.
The door was locked and solid enough to discourage kicking
it down. With the beating they'd put on me, and the noise it
would make, they'd be on me before I burst free.

They'd moved me off the casino grounds. The corner
window looked over the Broadbeach mall, where a brass
band played in the gazebo. Harried shoppers hustled
between stores and an abundance of restaurants. The scents
of working kitchens proved distracting, given my hunger. A

mouthwatering melange of Thai food, Indian, Yum Cha, and American barbecue set my stomach growling.

I finished walking the perimeter of the room, retreated to the red couch to wait.

Wesna unlocked the door and slid a plastic bag full of takeout through the gap. My mouth watered when I caught the rich scent of butter chicken, but I didn't crawl for it immediately. You can't accept gifts from the Other. First rule of doing business. Don't agree to a drink, don't eat their food, don't do shit that could leave you beholden to them.

Me, I was long past that stage. Whatever hooks I'd let Sabbath get beneath my skin, they would not get in deeper by eating curry. I resisted because there were strong odds of Wesna or Sabbath watching the room, paying attention to how I acted. I forced myself to stay on the couch, ignoring the food for a couple of minutes.

Then, when the rumble in my gut became an ache, I let myself give in.

I ate fast, eager to fill my empty stomach. The food sat heavy, a stone weighing me down, and I dragged my ass back to the sofa to digest. Stretched each limb, testing where the limits of my pain and how far I could push myself.

Wesna didn't lie—they'd been real careful to leave me functional. My jaw hurt like hell after the beating Randall put on it, and my ribs were a black mess of bruising. But nothing had been broken, which meant I'd heal in days instead of months.

Faster, if I broke down and tapped the Gloom to help, but I preferred not to do that. The price was too damn high.

Sabbath reappeared after sunset. Wesna followed on his heels, passed the boss a can of Coke. He popped it open and held it to me, waited for me to take it. I stared at the drink, stared at him. "It ain't poisoned," he said. "That wouldn't be smart."

I took the Coke and swallowed. After a long day in the pressure cooker Sabbath called an apartment, the chilly bite of the cola against my teeth was pretty close to heaven.

"I don't buy it," Sabbath said. "Sixteen years, Murphy. That's how long I've wanted to get my hands on you, all that time dreaming about paying you back for all your little betrayals. In all that time, the one thing that galled me was the knowledge your soul was safe. Even as a teen, you were smart enough to guard that and refused to let me have it."

"And now I'm here, all grown up, offering it to you on a platter?"

"Precisely," Sabbath said. "It's not the kind of move you make, Murphy. As Wesna is fond of saying, it seems... unprofessional."

"Me and professional stopped talking a couple of weeks back," I said. "The moment we fucked the Wotan hit."

"Please, I don't believe that. If you parted ways with Danny Roark, he'd come after me with both guns blazing. It's the only way to save your life. So you're playing a long game, Murphy. I can taste it."

I nodded, then winced. My jaw still ached. "Ragnarök," I said.

"The twilight of the gods?"

"My guess is that's an imperfect translation, given it came from your side of the Gloom," I said. "You know how these things go. Some ancient entity has a vision about destroying the world, tries to project it into the brains of some dumb shit vikings. They interpret it as the end of the gods, because they don't have any other word for it."

"I assume you have a point, Murphy."

"That same thing, in the deep Gloom, courted Michael Wotan," I said. "He was trying to kick off Ragnarök when me and Roark put him down, 'cept we fucked the job and his cult seems to think everything's on schedule. One of the possible ends of the world is coming, and I kinda doubt it's the apocalypse your kind wants to win out."

Sabbath thought that over. Broke into a grin. "And that's what brought you back?"

"That, among other things."

"Very well." Sabbath's smile belonged on a predator. A big cat. A shark. Something fast and efficient and utterly sure of itself. "You don't expect to survive what's coming?"

"Not really."

"And your soul?"

"Is doomed either way," I said. "Better the devil you know."

Sabbath shook his head. He stood and walked over to the window, arms folded as he glared at the people below. "When you first returned, I intended to use you like a tool. Eliminate those who opposed me, from the irritating to the dangerous. You failed me in that, but I've dug around. We've confirmed what you've told me about Thirteen, about his connections and his... alliances." The last word slipped out in a wary, sibilant hiss. "But I don't just want your soul, Murphy, I'd prefer your service. I'll help you stop Thirteen, because that's good for business."

"Great."

"I wasn't done." Sabbath rounded on me, smirk in place. "The price is servitude. You're one of my boys again, a willing soldier. I give you a name, and you kill them—no objections based on your morals. You'll partner with any demon I want you to work with, and I'll hear no complaints. If I want you to train a recruit, then you'll damn well train them. And you'll keep your soul intact through every dirty job, so I can enjoy the guilt it causes."

I forced myself upright. "I preferred you when you were vindictive, Sabbath."

"I preferred you when you were a punk," Sabbath said.

"You didn't attempt to play me, Murphy, back when you were a kid."

"I had nothing worth playing for," I said. "Otherwise I would have tried."

He held out his hand. I shook it, hating myself the whole time, and something dark settle over my soul. Sabbath's tender, ready to claim it when I screwed up enough that I passed over.

THE THIRD HIT

I climbed into SUV packed to the gills with monsters and started the drive up Tamborine Mountain. Randall in the driver's seat, Wesna riding shotgun. Me tucked into the back with three of Sabbath's thugs I didn't recognize. All sported the cruel, empty stares of demons who'd been residents of Earth long enough to dominate their human souls. The faces were different, but I recognized the crew: these were the guys Sabbath sent to deal with major threats, stripped of humanity and willing to cross lines those with a soul might balk at. A second SUV tailed us, more of Sabbath's operators loaded up and ready for trouble.

We sat in silence while the car took the mountain curves, stayed silent as the road straightened at the peak. From the top of Tamborine you could look out over the whole damn Gold Coast. It was night, and the lights glittered and shone like your own private fairyland. Beautiful, almost, from a distance. We rolled through the empty streets, passed farms with orchards full of avocados and limes. Pulled up a half-click short of the property identified as Thirteen's personal fortress.

From the road, it seemed like a peaceful area. Nothing suggesting a cult would flourish there, let alone fortify. A double-story house ringed by groves of apple trees on three sides, with the fourth side up against a cliff that looked out over the Coast. Well-maintained and in good nick. The kind of place that attracted a price-tag above the means of your average cowls-and-chants crew.

We stood around the cars and geared up. Randall unearthed my SIG and handed it back to me, along with a knife and three clips of ammo. The demons carried shotguns, loaded up on sidearms. Everyone waited for Randall to signal the advance, climbed over the fence at his nod. We crept through the orchard, all silent. All professional. Every hundred meters Randall would hold up a fist, bring us to a halt. One demon would peel off from the pack, disappear into the shadows, and when they reappeared, there was blood on their hands. Sentry positions. Wandering guards. Sabbath's blunt instrument understood their job. They worked quiet, and bloody.

We made it through the trees. Split up as we approached the house. Thirteen wasn't stupid. Floodlights faced out over the exterior grounds. Motions sensors attached to them, so they'd go up if someone tried to approach. More security than your average suburbanite goes for. Not even the kind of thing wealthy Tamborine commuter would write off as normal. It didn't matter. This was the Gold Coast. Eccentricities were a regular deal, embraced as little streaks of local color.

Wesna and Randall crouched beside me, studied the set-up. Wesna put a finger to her lips, pointed to three spots around the house. I squinted, saw the moving shadows. More guards. More cultists, standing vigil. Randall signaled the rest of the crew, and the demons melted into the darkness.

One by one the sentries disappeared. Sabbath's team avoided the lights, excelled at bypassing wards and cut throats. All lookouts eliminated inside of ten minutes, no alarm raised. Randall and Wesna shared a tight nod, and Wesna touched my arm. We all understood what came next, but I wasn't looking forward to it.

Randall reached into the darkness, gathered it together until it thickened. A portal to the Gloom, tethered to the real world.

Then Wesna stepped through, pulling me in behind her.

The transition between our plane of existence and the frigid currents of the Gloom is like the early stages of drowning. First the cold hit, then all sensation spiraling out of control, like getting sucked beneath the surface by a strong rip. The pair of us whipped around by the wild eddies and tides of the place. The realization that you no longer possessed any mass. Mortals don't belong in the in the Gloom. All we saw, based on what Roark taught me, were vague impressions of our surroundings. Shadow, indistinct reflections of the places we'd encountered in the real world.

Wesna dragged me behind her, the grip around my arm cinched tight. I closed my eyes, tried not to scream. Let the cold darkness wash over me.

Then it was over, Wesna dragging me through a second portal, wrestling me free of the Gloom that didn't want to release me back into the world. Warm hands held mine, movement returning to my fingers. My ragged, panicked breathing grew steady.

I pushed myself upright. We'd emerged by the mansion, under the motion sensors. Tight as we could get via Gloom, given Thirteen's defenses. A laundry entrance three meters down. I inched past Wesna, broke out the lock picks. Worked slow, cautious, to keep the noise down. The lock clicked, too loud for my taste. I eased the door open, registered the push of Thirteen's wards. Those gave way after I dug the soul cage out of my pocket, pressed the reliquary with Wotan's spirit up against the intangible barrier.

The bullet bucked in my fingers, Wotan's essence

awakened by contact with his follower's magic. I gripped it tight, forced it to submit. Held it there until the turmoil eased, the soul going dormant again inside its prison.

Randall slipped past me, into the house. Wesna followed, crouched low, wincing a little as though she expected the wards to catch her. We were in the laundry, heading into the kitchen. There were two cultists there, loitering. Both were dead by the time I entered, their necks twisted into modern art by the demon's furious strength.

Wesna looked at me, eyebrow raised. I gestured. Up. The Raven Cult always chose up. They liked their rituals close to the sky.

We heard the chanting before we saw them. They were on the upper deck, this long expanse of woodwork that jutted over the cliff. I figure Thirteen bought the house just for that wide veranda, the open space exposed to the night air. A place where he could do the things that needed doing.

They'd carted a granite slab up there, surrounded it with twelve men in dark robes and deep hoods. Thirteen stood in the center of it all, the false bullet on a plinth of stone. Nora lingered at the edge of the circle, gnawing on a fingernail. Still wearing the oversized shirt from the safe house, the borrowed pair of Langford's jeans. They'd armed her, left her to serve as a guard dog. A short, dressed-down punk with a big Winchester pump action.

Thirteen raised his hands, palms open to the sky. I didn't recognize his chant, but that didn't mean much. Thirteen's mentor, Michael Wotan, prayed to entities older than anything I'd studied, things that slumbered in the deep parts of the Gloom waiting for a return to earth. Their worship involved languages most folks considered dead, and knowing them was always Roark's part of the job.

They'd tethered themselves, all thirteen men. Tapped into

the umbral currents of the Gloom and drawn on its power, preparing to invest it in the nine millimeter round at the heart of their ritual. The energy hanging in the air like a static charge. The hair on my arms stood to attention and the tether marks itched like crazy. They were going for big magic, the kind of shit most sorcerers tried to stay away from.

Easiest way to kill a cultist is disrupting his rituals, letting the Gloom feed on him instead of his preferred victim. On this scale, the challenge became figuring out what to disturb. With so much energy floating about, it could suck in anyone trapped in the backlash. I glanced at Wesna, caught her short nod. The kind of rift they were looking to open tended to be bad news, regardless of whether you were mortal or Other.

The ritual hit a fever pitch, dark flames appearing around the bullet. Thirteen's chanting rose towards a crescendo, eyes rolling back in his head. They were waiting for that energy to crack the wards on the reliquary, free their leader from his tiny purgatory. Instead, it blew the fake soul cage to dust, reducing the lead and steel and powder down to component atoms.

Thirteen glared at the results of his magic. Realized the switch and howled, turning on Nora. She reacted like you'd expect, switched over to self-preservation mode. Leveled the shotgun at his chest.

I nodded to Wesna, stepped out of cover and onto the balcony. The SIG kicked in my hands, targeting the closest member of Thirteen's ritual circle. He pitched forward, blood spilling from a hole in his shoulder. The magic they were channeling bucked, forcing the others to focus on getting it under control. Thirteen registered the kick, glanced in my direction.

Nora Otto seized upon the distraction and fired the big Remington into Thirteen's chest.

The sorcerer staggered. Blood oozed out the front of a robe torn to tatters by Nora's buckshot. Magic kept him upright.

All the energy he channeled, unsure where to go after the bullet disintegrated, found its home in his flesh. Thirteen advanced on Nora and smashed a fist into her cheek.

Wesna and Randall burst into motion, working their way around the circle. They snapped necks and cut throats. Buried knives deep in the stomachs of those who resisted dying. Any semblance of restraint evaporated and wild magic set things alight. The wooden landing. One cultist's hair. Parts of Thirteen's body. I leveled the SIG. Fired twice. Thirteen charged me, knocked me to the floor. The pistol skittered out of my grasp and Thirteen's foot caught me in the ribs.

He lost control. Fire ripped along his arms, burnt away his black t-shirt, and his eyes became dark chasms, deeper than any demon's gaze. Thirteen burned through energy fast, and soon it'd burn out on him, but until then it gave him options. Bolstered speed and strength, healing wounds at an accelerated pace. He swung at me, more magic than muscle. I ducked under and the impact took out a chunk of the balustrade. Wood shattered beneath his fist, showering me with splinters.

He rocked back, guard raised, but I didn't bother with a counter. Nothing I hit him with would do much more than annoy him.

Thirteen moved with inhuman speed, and the flames on his arms burned hotter and higher. I figured he ran on anger, his thwarted rage giving the Gloom focus and allowing him to channel through the searing pain. The sorcerer jumped at me, clawing for my throat. The heat singed my cheek as I scrambled out of his reach. If he locked in the choke, I knew I was dead.

His fury would burn out and kill him, but it wasn't happening fast enough.

I kicked at him, tried to push free. Got lucky when his head jerked back, Wesna coming up from the rear and hooking fingers into his nose.

She punched him in the face, put all her strength behind it. As a demon, she hit harder than I ever could. Thirteen's jaw snapped sideways with the blow, splattering blood as his mouth busted open.

Wesna stood over him, breathing heavy. Thirteen rose and rounded on her, roaring with laughter.

I dove for the SIG, rolled with the momentum. Came to a halt against the balcony railings, jarring my shoulder hard. Didn't matter. I brought the pistol up and fired. Caught him up high, middle of the back. Enough damage to start overwhelming his magic, force him to call on more.

Thirteen advance on Wesna faltered, and I emptied the weapon. Five rounds. Dead center. Thirteen teetered, still burning, unwilling to fall. Wesna lunged, and he lashed out at her, backhanded her to the floor. I slammed the fresh clip home as he turned, bearing down on me.

That's the mistake that killed him. I fired two shots, kept Thirteens focus on me, and Wesna launched herself at his back. The impact knocked Thirteen off-balance, and Wesna's hammered his neck with both fists. It snapped and Thirteen dropped to one knee, anger diverting his attention to the immediate threat.

My final shot caught Thirteen in the side of the head. There wasn't sufficient rage in the world to keep him upright after the mess that made, and no healing would repair the damage before the magic burnt out.

Weans hauled me off the floor, held me up as we surveyed the carnage. The remnants of Thirteen's cult fled, desperate to escape the battlefield. All of them learned, the hard way, about Wesna's back-up team lurking outside the house.

Wesna studied at the chaos, mouth tight with satisfaction. She pointed to a huddled, bloodied figure slumped by the ritual granite block. "What about her, then?"

I nodded. Raised the SIG. Nora looked up at me, through

her curls. Her lips bloody, smiling, defiant. Still just a little bit punk. "You going to kill me, Murphy?"

I thought about that. Finger on the trigger. Screams came out of the darkness. Plenty of Thirteen's cultists around, running into demons in the dark. So many assholes in need of killing, but I'd lost the stomach for it.

EXILED

We packed into the SUVs for the trip down the mountain. Randall drove, unhappy as hell. Wesna rode shotgun, mouth pulled into a grim line. It was six in the morning. Sunlight coming over the horizon. The rest of the demons were up at the house, eliminating any signs of our involvement. Not all of them, I figured. They'd keep some traces of my presence there. Insurance, in case I did something stupid. *Oh officer, about that cold case. Have you looked into this asshole who left DNA all around the scene...*

Nora sat in the seat beside me. Bound and gagged. Zip ties on the wrists and ankles. Old rags stuffed into her mouth. Randall offered to kill her for me, couldn't understand why I told him to back off. Wesna did. She didn't like it, but she understood. No matter how much demon they squeezed into her, there were parts that remained stubbornly human.

We rolled through the national park, through the backstreets of Nerang where the estates and the prize-homes sat side-by-side with industrial parks. Sunday morning. Quiet and sleepy, in this part of town. It's the surfers who rose early. I needed to remember that. Get the hell away from the beach.

We pulled into the parking lot at Nerang Station, empty as

hell in the wee hours. I let myself out, went around to open Nora's door. Wesna was already there. She looked me in the eye, wanting to be sure I knew what I was doing.

I nodded. Produced a knife. Cut the zip-ties binding Nora's arms and legs. She climbed out, eyes full of fire, but Wesna's presence kept her from taking a swing at me. Nora, on her own, might have had sufficient fury to beat the crap out of me, but she'd spent that anger and it hadn't panned out. My side won and her side lost.

That's the problem with attempting to change your corner of the world—it takes a lot out of you once you realize that you're helpless.

"You can't remain here," I said. "You're sure as hell not going to win, if you pick a fight with Sabbath."

I offered her a roll of bills. Salvage from the cult's lair. Nora looked at the money. "You seriously think I'm willing to run, Murphy?"

"I'm hoping you'll try."

She chewed on that for a few seconds. Took the cash off my hands. About six hundred. Enough to put some distance between us.

"Spend some quality time in Melbourne," I said. "You'll like it there. Good coffee. Lots of bars. It shouldn't take long to set yourself up."

Nora's eyes narrowed. "I don't need your advice."

I held her stare with my own. "This isn't letting you go. This is giving you a head start. If Sabbath still wants you dead, he'll send people. Make sure you've got someplace you can defend, or you've hooked up with someone that'll force him think twice about going after you."

"I can't believe you're doing this."

"You'd prefer death?"

"Maybe." She looked me in the eye, and I could see she wasn't joking. A part of her hated leaving. Loathed giving in.

"I'm not like you, Murphy. Running's never been my style. I'd rather stay and fight."

I nodded, slowly. "You can try that."

Nora glanced towards the car. Randall glaring at her. Wesna standing there, arms folded, expression stern.

"No, I really can't." She leant in, kissed me on the cheek. "Welcome home. Not sure I ever said that."

I stood there, saying nothing. Wesna cleared her throat, the noise close to a snarl.

"Right then." Nora affected a triumphant grin that was ninety percent bravado. "Fuck you all, then."

Nora held her chin high all the way to the station. Bought a ticket that'd take her north. Brisbane, first. God knows where after that. Somewhere far, far from the Coast if she was smart, and I hoped to hell she was. I climbed back into the car. We all hunkered down, waiting. Unwilling to depart until we'd seen Nora climb aboard and leave the city.

Then, when the train pulled away, and the station was empty, Randall gunned the engine and reversed us out of the lot.

WANT TO KNOW WHAT HAPPENS NEXT?

FROST: The Second Book in the Gold Coast Ragnarök Trilogy

Rule one for surviving Ragnarök?
Don't piss off a Valkyrie.

Ex-hitman Keith Murphy sold his services to a demon in order to stop an apocalyptic cult. Now he's stuck fighting a gang way against a local biker gang who knows far too much about magic for a pack of mortals. A routine hit turns into a mystery, and that mystery leads to a series of deaths with a very unexpected source. *Something* has crossed over from the darkest parts of the Gloom, and it seems like Keith sold his soul to delay Ragnarök instead of stopping it.

The last, long winter frost before the end of the world is

setting in, and the only man who can stop it is a pissed-off, well-armed assassin with nothing left to lose

Read on for a taste of *Frost*...

FROST PREVIEW

The hit on Eli Penny went sour at 12:01 AM, right after a cool spring Monday gave way to Tuesday morning. Problem was, we didn't know it yet, so we kept on playing it like things were going smooth. I crouched in the Sailboat Cafe's kitchen, a loaded Mossberg shotgun clenched in a two-handed grip. Ready to back up my partner, Finn, when Penny finally arrived.

I could hear Finn pacing the floorboards of the dining room. Heavy footsteps rendered louder by his penchant for motorcycle boots. Finn's role in the plan was simple: lure Penny into the café and get him talking. Stay clear of the kitchen door. I'd step out and pull a trigger, and Eli Penny would bother our boss no more.

Unfortunately Finn's nervous pacing suggested his human half wasn't as comfortable with the scheme as the demon who shared custody of the biker's mortal flesh. I'd seen it before in Sabbath's newer guys, the restless irritation when the prick of a mortal conscience comes up against the new inhabitant's desires.

Part of me almost felt sorry for Penny, because Finn's

demonic tenant would make him pay for those little moments of human frailty when the violence started.

A bad feeling settled over me as the seconds ticked by. I couldn't place the reason: I figured the job for a cakewalk, even if Finn Caylin was equal parts amateur liability and demonically possessed wildcard. Finn could fuck up, and odds were things would still come up roses for us.

I mean, hell, Penny and his Rebels weren't supposed to know he'd joined up with Sabbath's crew. They sure as hell shouldn't know what Sabbath's crew really *were*.

That's the problem with working for demons, I guess. They get so goddamn cocky when they're picking fights with mortals, and I got cocky right along with them.

There was a bar out front, and Finn helped himself to a bottle of Absolut. Unscrewed the cap and hammered down the first mouthful like he wanted to quench an internal fire. Poor bastard didn't yet know how little alcohol affects the demonically possessed, so I doubted the vodka did much for him. The clock ticked past 12:10, and Eli Penny was officially late.

The Sailboat's kitchen wasn't the most comfortable place to wait for a target. They built it galley-style, a single counter and a stovetop. Just enough space to cook bar food at speed, and toast the occasional sandwich. The grease-traps lent a thick aroma to the tight confines, and the taps leaked into the sink. Water plinked against the stainless-steel basin five inches from my head. Regular as a metronome, each drop followed by three seconds of silence as the next beaded on the rim of the faucet.

At 12:16 we caught the sound of Eli Penny's Harley approaching. Finn heard it first, human senses honed to a predatory acuity by the demon's presence beneath his skin. His gait changed, and the Absolut returned to its shelf behind the bar. He called a warning to me seconds before the growl of the engine registered.

Penny came down Thrower Drive and pulled into the Sailboat's shared lot, his bike rolling to a halt in front of the bait and tackle place next door. I flexed my fingers and adjusted my grip on the Mossberg. Inhaled and exhaled, counting to three each time, staying cool despite the adrenaline flowing through my system. Outside, the idling engine of Penny's motorcycle pushed away all other sounds. The snarl of it blocked the dripping tap and the clomp of Finn's angry gait.

I took a second breath. Three seconds in, three seconds out. Penny's engine continued to rumble. Finn's silhouette flashed past the circular window set into the kitchen door.

I counted another three seconds.

And another.

Eli Penny's motorcycle engine showed no signs of cutting off, and my bad feeling turned into a strong suspicion the hit was going wrong. I got traction on the cold tile floor, rose to my feet with the Mossberg held high. The dining room of the Sailboat was empty except for the tables and stacked chairs. Finn was out on the wide deck, raising his voice to invite Penny in for a drink. Focused on the plan, luring his ex-boss inside so my shotgun could end his life.

They came at me while Finn and Penny were jawing at each other, trying to play it cool. I caught sight of looming shadow passing by kitchen window, registered the creak of a floorboard as someone big and sneaky made their way along the Sailboat's back deck. Out front, Finn called Eli Penny a damned suspicious cunt, which seemed to coax the other man into accepting the offer of a drink.

Finn strolled back to the bar with the jaunty step of a guy convinced he'd done good, unaware of the shitstorm bearing down on him. I repositioned the Mossberg to cover the rear door, caught the soft click of a crowbar being wedged against the doorjamb. These boys weren't going for subtle. I was betting they'd come in hard-and-fast when they got the signal. Out front, Eli Penny rolled across the front deck, stopping at the open doorway leading into the dining room.

The biker's big, rough voice asked a single question: "You really think we wouldn't know, Finn?"

Then a gun spat twice in the tight confines of the café. Shots fired at 12:24, and it flushed away any hope of the hit going right.

Judging by the sound, Penny came armed with a small calibre handgun. The kind of weapon it's easy to conceal when your target's expecting you to cause trouble. With Finn's new, demonically possessed strength and metabolism, close range shooting from a .22 was more likely to piss him off than deal grievous injury.

Meanwhile, I'd scored a few playmates of my own...

Frost and the other books in the Keith Murphy sequence are available now. Order it direct from Brain Jar Press, find it in your favourite store, or pick up a copy of the Gold Coast Ragnarök to get them hole trilogy in a single volume!

ABOUT THE AUTHOR

PETER M. BALL is an author, publisher, and RPG gamer whose love of speculative fiction emerged after exposure to *The Hobbit*, *Star Wars*, David Lynch's *Dune*, and far too many games of *Dungeons and Dragons* before the age of 7. He's spent the bulk of his life working as a creative writing tutor, with brief stints as a performance poet, gaming convention organiser, online content developer, non-profit arts manager, GenreCon convenor, and d20 RPG publisher.

He's the author of the Miriam Aster series and the Keith Murphy Urban Fantasy Thrillers, three short story collections, and more stories, articles, poems, and RPG material than he'd care to count. He's the brain-in-charge at Brain Jar Press, and resides in Brisbane, Australia, with his partner and a very affectionate cat.

Want to get in touch?
www.petermball.com

Or reach out to Peter on your favourite Social Media platforms:

facebook.com/PeterMBall

twitter.com/PeterMBall

instagram.com/PeterMBall

goodreads.com/PeterMBall

patreon.com/PeterMBall

ALSO BY PETER M. BALL

SHORT STORY COLLECTIONS

The Birdcage Heart & Other Strange Tales

Not Quite The End Of the World Just Yet: Short Stories & Strange Futures

These Strange & Magic Things: Short Stories

KEITH MURPHY URBAN FANTASY THRILLERS

Exile

Frost

Crusade

MIRIAM ASTER NOVELLAS

Horn

Bleed

BRAIN JAR PRESS SHORT FICTION LAB

The Early Experiments

Winged, With Sharp Teeth

8 Minutes Of Usable Daylight

A White Cross Beside A Lonely Road

One Last First Date Before The End Of The World

Shedding Skins

ESSAYS

You Don't Want To Be Published & Other Things Nobody Tells You When You First Start Writing

THANK YOU FOR BUYING
THIS BRAIN JAR PRESS BOOK

To receive special offers, bonus content, and info on new releases and other great reads, sign up for our newsletters.

To get more from the author, Peter M. Ball, you can sign up for his newsletter at PeterMBall.com

To get the latest updates form the publisher, Brain Jar Press, you can sign up at BrainJarPress.com